Writers of the Flames

A Writers' Rooms Community Anthology

Ross T. Byers & Erin Casey, eds.

First edition, 2022.
The Writers' Rooms
Iowa City, IA
welcome@thewritersrooms.org

Cover design is by: Erin Casey

Cover art: The Rock of Salvation (1837) by Samuel Colman. Original from The MET Museum.

ISBN: 978-0-578-38668-3

To the writers of the community who make
The Writers' Rooms possible…thank you.

Table of Contents

Introduction

Dear Reader, thank you for your support of The Writers' Rooms (TWR)! By picking up this book, you have joined our creative community. This book is our way to celebrate you and to thank everyone for helping our dream of the Rooms come to life.

TWR is an organization which endeavors to create a safe, inclusive community for all writers. We believe that everyone has a wealth of knowledge and a story to share. In our Rooms we bring both to the table. These community-led meetings include a myriad of craft discussions, prompts, lessons, and time to socialize and write. Our events, which are usually held in conjunction with local businesses and libraries, offer a safe space in which to meet other members of your local writing community. Due to COVID-19, some of our Rooms have remained virtual, while others are meeting in person. You can find the most recent updates at thewritersrooms.org and in our monthly newsletter.

Our Rooms would not exist were it not for the incredible writers throughout the creative corridor. We've watched new writers learn from seasoned minds. Authors with writer's block have found a way to flourish and venture into their literary world once again. Most importantly, people have found a Room to call home, a place where they feel safe to share their voice and find help when they struggle.

The stories, poetry, and art you're about to experience are from our community. We are writers helping writers who endeavor to share each others' voices. We chose the theme of fire for this anthology to continue our elemental journey.

Just remember, no matter where you are in your writing journey, you are never alone. You have a community waiting for you.

Best,
The Publishing Committee

Special Thanks

We wish to thank everyone who was involved in the creation of this anthology.

Rich Brown
Ross T. Byers
Erin Casey
Nick Goodman
Derek Maurer
Megan Walsh
Kat Weglarz

Untitled 1
Spike Dawkins

The Death of the Dreaming Wind
Rachel J. Sharkey

Gather around the fire and I will tell you a story…

***

In the deepest parts of the world, where the snow never melts and the sun can never quite reach the very top of the sky, the North Wind lives in a glittering castle made of ice. The North Wind is a quiet wind, and would prefer to never leave his quiet castle and its soft grounds.

But the North Wind is a dutiful wind, so he ventures out when he must and walks around the world on heavy, quiet feet. The North Wind is the God of Winter, because he is the God of Rest, and Dreams, and of All Quiet Things. But the North Wind is also the God of Winter because that is when he must work, and the North Wind hates to work. The North Wind is a God of Rest, and for that we love him, but he is also a God of Death, yet we love him for that too.

But quietly. Always quietly.

***

The North Wind blows around the mountain peaks and through the foothills and whistles over the prairies, and comes to a town that is quite like yours and quite near, but too far away to visit.

Walking through the cobbled streets of this town is a Little Girl who has nowhere to sleep. She wanders the streets, selling matches and hopes that if she sells enough, the foreman of the matchstick factory will turn a blind eye to her sleeping just inside the factory door.

It is unfortunate that she is out on the same night as the North Wind. The North Wind is a cold wind and her coat is thin, and bought when she was an even smaller girl than she is now.

She is still a very small girl.

***

The Little Girl sells a match to a woman walking home with her daughter while the North Wind gusts around them. There is nothing like the North Wind to make a person long for fire. But their coats are so much longer and thicker than the Little Girl's. The North Wind backs away from the Little Girl and leaves to gust around the eaves and the steeples.

The North Wind is not a kind wind, but he wishes he was.

****

The Little Girl offers matches to a tradesman leading a horse, and to an elderly lady carrying parcels, and to a factory worker, heading home. But no one buys one. Perhaps she would have been better off under the cold and watchful eye of the North Wind. But perhaps not.

Who can tell these things for certain?

****

The sun is getting lower in the sky now and it is getting colder, even though the North Wind is staying carefully up by the eaves and rattling the shingles. The Little Girl is shivering. It makes it hard to hold the matches when she tries to offer them to a banker in a fur-lined coat. The banker shoves past her, as if she is not even there, and nearly knocks her down.

He should have been more careful.

****

The sun is all the way down to the horizon now, the light is making the windows glow like candles. The Little Girl does not have any candles. Only matches. It's so cold now, and getting dark. She lights just one match. The light of the match is not much. Just enough to see the cobbles under her feet. But she looks into the light of the match and dreams about having a warm coat like the banker's. She imagines walking down the street in a long, red coat with a deep hood all lined with fur.

The North Wind can see her dreams, but he can't make her warm.

****

It is dark now. The Sun has laid down below the horizon for the night. The Moon presides over the scene. The Moon, and the North

Wind, who is wrapped around the church steeple. The beams of the belfry groan when he shakes them. The bell ringers pull on their gloves. The Little Girl, down below, has no gloves to pull on and her hands are getting numb. She lights another match, just to warm up her hands. One match is not enough to warm anything else. She watches it flicker and dreams about running in the snow, and not being cold because she has warm thick gloves and heavy boots. A young doctor, walking toward the hospital to work, stops to watch the light of the match. But he doesn't buy one.

Perhaps he should have known better.

***

The North Wind weeps, watching the Little Girl. The cold, clinging snow that falls drives the last few people walking down the street indoors. The Little Girl used to love the snow when she could watch it fall from safely inside. She ducks into a doorway and lights another match. It is not enough to warm her, it is barely enough to see by. It is just a scrap of fire. Of warmth. She dreams about a warm breeze which would warm her all the way through.

The Spring Winds are still far away, they are not listening.

***

The North Wind hates to work. But it is too late now. He must. The Little Girl will not be sleeping inside the matchstick factory door tonight. Perhaps the foreman will wonder after her. But perhaps not. She was a very small girl, after all. The North Wind, who is a God of Winter and a God of Rest, is also a God of Death, and so he must take the Little Girl away.

But he doesn't want to.

***

The snowflakes obscure the presiding Moon. The Little Girl has finally stopped. She has stopped by the house of the owner of the matchstick factory, although she does not know it. She tries to light one last match, to keep going. In her heart, she is full of fire. But she is cold and her hands are numb and the matches all catch light and scatter onto the ground. Most of them fall in the snow. But one falls against the walls of the house, the fine wooden walls of the house of the owner of the matchstick factory. The thick, soft snowflakes extinguish the matches, but they are not enough to put out the flames that are shimmering and dancing up the side of the house.

The fire is so fast and so light on its feet and so very hungry.

***

In the morning when the flames are sated, when the firemen have finally extinguished the coals where the fine house once stood, they will ask themselves why that cold North Wind, the one they had heard rattling around the eaves that night, had not stopped the fire. But the North Wind did not see the fire. He was not there. He had gathered the Little Girl into his arms and he had gone away.

They had gone home.

***

In the deepest parts of the world, where the snow never melts but where the sun sparkles on the snow, the Dreaming Wind lives in a glittering castle made of ice. She runs carefree through the snow in a long, red coat, heavy boots and fur gloves.

A warm breeze follows behind her wherever she goes.

The Phoenix and the Dragon
Ross T. Byers

As the blade slashed her throat, Seraphina thought if there was one thing she knew from experience, it was that dying always sucked.

The young boy had been brought to her weeping and bleeding from a five-inch gash in his forearm. Dr. Seraphina Lawson had seen many worse wounds in her time, but she sympathized with the kid. At such a young age getting hurt in a way that required stitches could seem apocalyptic. She was adroit at suturing wounds, even with the kid's mother watching the whole quick procedure hawk-like through watering eyes. The woman shed at least as many tears as her son.

After Sera finished she produced a bright red cherry sucker from one of her lab coat pockets. The cellophane wrapper, printed on one side with a smiley face, crinkled as the boy took it from her hand.

"That was nice," said the mother, drying her eyes with what had to be her hundredth tissue. "Billy, what do we say?"

"Thank you."

"It was nothing," said Sera.

She had been saving the candy for herself as a post-rounds treat, but the kid looked like he needed it more. She walked the patient and his mother back out of the room, stifling a yawn as soon as their backs were to her. Ten hours at the hospital and a couple more to go until she was done. There was probably more caffeine than blood running through her veins. She closed her eyes and entertained a brief fantasy about going back to her tiny apartment and collapsing into bed.

When she opened her eyes she spotted him walking through the hospital's waiting area. He still had a limp. He always would. It was a shock, and a rush of memories and emotions washed through her—fire and blood, pain and passion. He was heading towards the exit, passing under the glowing crimson EXIT sign, the tip of his cane rapping on the floor. He hadn't noticed her, eyes fixed on the doors, his objective, but now that she'd seen him she couldn't just let him leave without saying hello.

Seraphina glided through the throng of those waiting to be seen and said, "Robert, hey."

He stopped just in front of the doors and turned his green eyes to her. A smile lit up his face. Well, that was a relief.

"That you, Lawson?" he said. "Wow, it's good to see you. How long has it been?"

"I don't know, years," said Seraphina.

"Too long," he said, shifting his cane to his other hand, putting the right out for a shake.

She took it. His palm was dry and strangely warm. A little thrill sparked in her belly at the contact. God, apparently the years had done nothing to douse the torch she carried. She let go, and the air cooling her hand was torture.

"So, you work here?" asked Robert.

"Yeah, it's Doctor Lawson now."

"That's awesome. I know it was your dream."

"Yeah, it's great. I mean, it's hectic and I don't get enough sleep and I managed to rack up a huge amount of debt, but it's what I always wanted. How about you? What are you doing?"

"Lawyer," said Robert. "I'm an associate over at my dad's old firm, which, you know, is totally nepotism, but I'm benefiting from it so I'd appreciate it if you could keep that between us."

Seraphina laughed and said, "Deal."

Robert nodded to a nearby empty chair and said, "Mind if I sit down?"

"No, not at all."

Robert sat with a relieved sigh, stretching out his right leg. The prosthetic peeked out between his shoe and the hem of his trousers. She winced and looked back up at his face. The smile was still there, which was encouraging.

"Just came in for a readjusting of the old peg leg," said Robert, rapping his knuckles on the prosthetic. "Sometimes the meat gets sore, but sitting helps."

"I'm sorry about—"

"Don't even start. It wasn't in any way your fault. You saved my life, Lawson. I owe you everything. I'll owe you forever."

"You could start paying that debt by calling me Sera."

Robert laughed. "Sorry, old habit. Sera it is, then. If there's anything else I can do for you, please let me know."

"Well, I'd love to catch up. Maybe over a cup of coffee?"

"Oh, for sure. Are you free tomorrow?"

"Actually, yeah."

"There's this great little place off Ashland. Give me your number and I'll text you the address."

Robert pulled a sleek, cutting-edge phone from a pocket in his slacks. Seeing it made Sera slightly ashamed of her own phone, which was a few years past its prime. Even with tuition assistance from the military she had racked up a mountain of debt to pay for med school. It didn't leave much of a budget for upgrades. Still, she was happy to make the exchange.

"I've got to get back to my rounds," she said, brushing a loose strand of fiery hair away from her face. "It was so good running into you."

"It was," said Robert, standing up. "Coffee tomorrow."

"I'm looking forward to it."

Sera watched him leave, and finished her rounds on cloud nine.

It was late at night when Seraphina left the hospital. She turned and walked down the dark street towards the El station. Heat that had been absorbed over the course of the summer day radiated from the surrounding concrete. She was almost there when a strong hand shot out of the murky mouth of an alley and pulled her in.

Her assailant threw her back against the wall. Stars exploded in her vision as her head bounced off the rough bricks. He waved a knife in front of Sera's face but she couldn't take her eyes off the lice crawling in his grizzled beard.

Breath like rancid meat gusted against her face as he said, "Give me your purse!"

He tugged on her handbag, and even dazed Sera knew the best thing would be to let him take it. Out of pure reflex she clutched it, played tug-of-war. With a grunt he grabbed a fistful of her hair and cut her throat, dragging the blade through her carotid arteries and trachea.

The purse fell from her spasming fingers. Magma-hot blood sprayed from the wound, coating his lower face and drenching his shirt. He screamed as it burned through his flesh, his clothes bursting into flames upon contact. Seraphina's corpse crumpled, clothes blazing where her blood spilled over them. Dime- and quarter-sized spots of the pavement between them glowed and liquefied, sending up streamers of acrid smoke. The assailant fell back against the opposite wall as golden flames spread with unnatural rapidity over his body, turning him into a column of fire.

He did not scream for long.

The twin blazes flared then winked out like snuffed candles. Gray-white ash drifted through the air. The assailant had burned away, and in his place stood Seraphina, whole and unharmed, but naked. Two large streaks of soot, like wings, soiled the wall behind her. Where her previous body had fallen was a vaguely woman-shaped pile of ash swiftly losing its definition in the breeze. The clothes she had been wearing had gone up with the rest of her.

"Well, shit," she said.

On the whole it was probably better to be naked on the streets than dead, but it was an inconvenience. At least her purse had survived. She felt a momentary pang of guilt as she reached down for it. Yeah, the guy had killed her, but she never liked taking a life. Her fiery rebirths weren't something she had any control over, but she still felt a little responsible. Maybe if she'd done something differently they both could have lived.

Sera looked over her shoulder back at the mouth of the alleyway. She hoped no one had heard his screams or seen the fire, but this close to the El station she couldn't count on it. Clutching her purse to her body she shuffled deeper into the alley, away from the streetlights, keeping a careful eye on where she stepped. The last thing she wanted to do was cut her feet on broken glass.

Ahead, next to a reeking Dumpster, was a door. She tried to open it but it was locked. A box with numbered keys was set above the knob. Sighing, she extended an index finger and concentrated. A small, radiant flame sprang to life above her finger tip. Within moments she burned through the lock. She didn't like using the fire. There were those who were always keeping watch for supernatural disturbances—people, yes, and other things, too. Still, she'd already had a full flare-up, so a small flame wouldn't make a difference.

She stepped into a corridor with numbered doors lining both sides. Apartments. The floor was carpeted but felt gritty. To her immediate right was a door labeled "Stairs." She pushed through and took the descending flight. She smiled as she stepped into the laundry room, the grimy tile sending chills up her legs. Thankfully there was no one there, and a dryer was rumbling in the corner. She pulled a too-large tee shirt and pair of jeans from it and slipped into them. Her feet swam in the oversized socks; they weren't shoes, but they were better than nothing.

Feeling much better now that she was attired again, she slipped out the way she had come. Standing back at the mouth of the alley, she realized she didn't want to take the El while needing to hold up her pants with one hand and so pulled her phone from her purse and hailed a Lyft to take her home.

No matter how many times Robert Leblanc made the trip into the sewers he never got used to the smell. He held a handkerchief to his nose with his free hand while his other gripped the head of his cane. One of the acolytes walked ahead, hooded vermilion robes trailing. The tunnel they walked through was dry, isolated from the greater wastewater system: obscured, bribed out of memory, and erased from blueprints. The execrable stench still permeated the place, though.

They left the round sewer tunnel and entered an area of damp, roughly-hewn stone. Torches set in evenly spaced sconces gave off a flickering, smoky light. The red-gold scales of Robert's skin glittered, made visible by the firelight.

They stopped in front of the door to Robert's chamber, and he asked, "Do you know why Her Glorious Majesty sent for me so late at night?"

"No, sir," said the acolyte, head bowed so the hood obscured her face. "She only said to bring you right away."

Well, that was annoying. Robert had hoped for a decent night's sleep as he didn't want to show up to the coffee date with Sera with black bags under his eyes. Getting roused from his bed in the middle of the night and making the trip through the sewers for what may very well be a whim wasn't exactly conducive to looking his best, not to mention it would screw with his circadian rhythm. But such was his duty; he had been born, quite literally, to serve.

He dismissed the acolyte with a wave and entered his chamber. The torches and candles had already been lit. He laid aside his cane, shucked his pants, and removed the prosthetic leg. From the knot of scar tissue below his knee bloomed a reptilian lower limb, four clawed toes at the front and one at the heel. It glittered with the same red-gold scales as the rest of his body, and his black claws scratched shallow furrows in the rock as he flexed. Though it was difficult to walk with one digitigrade and one plantigrade foot, he managed just fine if he kept to a stately pace. He stripped off his shirt, letting his wings materialize and unfurl from his back. He took a deep breath, stoking the furnace that burned inside his chest like the heart of a star, and when he exhaled smoke billowed from his mouth and nostrils. It wasn't often he was able to let his inhuman side show, and he relished the chance.

After finding his balance on his mismatched legs, he donned his gold-trimmed saffron robes. He unlocked a small chest with an iron key that hung at all times from a leather cord about his neck, and from the chest withdrew the gold and ruby pendant that, along with the robes, was his badge of office. Thus properly attired, Robert braved the dragon's lair.

Breo Saighead watched him enter with eyes like napalm. Her long, sinuous body was curled around her enormous pile of gold and objets d'art, limbs and wings tucked gracefully. Her scales glittered like gold and rubies in wavy stripes that ran together in a molten stream. Wisps of smoke rose constantly from her nostrils and from between the fangs of her elongated, crocodilian mouth. A pair of black horns curved up and away from the back of her head like a lyre.

"It is good to see you, high priest," said the dragon. "Thank you for responding to my summons so quickly."

"It is my honor to serve you," said Robert.

He wended his way through stacks and piles of deeds, paper currency, and other flammable valuables that could not be kept among the main hoard mound. Along the sides of the spacious cavern, robed acolytes tended to the braziers that lit the room and to Breo Saighead's investment portfolio, charting the rise and fall of the stock markets on rugged, heat-resistant devices. Once within a respectful distance Robert knelt before the creature that was his liege, his goddess, and his mother.

"How may I serve?" he asked, keeping his eyes on the stone floor.

"I have sensed something tonight in the city above, fruit of my womb. An explosion of energy that is still rippling through the spirit world. I haven't felt something of this magnitude in some time, and the local spirits are all quite agitated. As my blood runs in your veins, and because you serve as my most trusted agent in the world above, I task you to investigate this matter. I need to know exactly what caused this, and, ideally, have you in place to stop it from happening again."

"So you think this poses a danger."

"Everything does," said Breo Saighead. "But, given how excited the fire spirits are, I'd say yes, this is exceptionally dangerous. I remember the last time fire got out of hand in the city."

"I will be cautious," said Robert. "Are there any specifics you can give me?"

"Not at the moment. Follow your instincts. Chances are the fire that burns inside you will respond to whatever was responsible, perhaps flare or become more intense."

Robert nodded; he'd felt something like that around Sera earlier, but he suspected the reason was more physiological than mystical. "May I ask a boon of you?"

"You may."

"There is a woman living in the city above. I crave your permission to court her."

"Is my little salamander feeling the first pangs of love? Is she human?"

"Most likely."

Breo Saighead stroked her slim chin with one clawed hand, gazing at Robert through narrowed eyes that gave her reptilian countenance a rather sly cast.

"I will allow it," said the dragon. "But you must promise, no matter how deeply you come to love this city woman, to always keep me first in your heart."

"I promise," said Robert, with only the faintest inkling it was already a lie.

Seraphina stepped inside the café, which was long and narrow, housed in a brick building. Early afternoon sunlight streamed in through the large front windows. She smiled when she saw Robert, already sitting at a table near an archway that led further back into the building. He gestured at the counter where a barista was taking orders and joined her in line.

"So, how do we decide who's paying?" asked Sera. "Should we compare debt?"

"I'll get it," said Robert. "Money isn't an issue for me right now."

Sera laughed. "That must be nice."

They ordered their coffees and sat at the table Robert had staked out. He was looking good in jeans and a button-down shirt open at the collar. She smoothed her dress, hoping she didn't look as frazzled as she felt. A side effect of getting killed and reborn was it made sleeping afterward difficult.

"So what did you do last night?" asked Robert.

"Oh, you know, I was pretty wiped after my rounds, so I just went home and slept. You?"

"Yeah, pretty much the same. Exciting, I know."

"I don't know about you, but I've already had pretty much all the excitement I need in my life."

"Which is why you work in a hospital."

"Okay, maybe it's not as sedate as being a lawyer. Unless you're a, what, defense attorney?"

"Nope, I specialize in contract law," said Robert. "It's not as sexy as being a trial lawyer, but I like it."

"So no dangerous clients, then."

"I wouldn't exactly say that."

"Oh, do tell," said Sera.

Robert looked away, scratching his cheek. "I'd better not."

"Playing it mysterious, I see. Well, at least you don't have to wrestle patients into restraints or chase down kids fleeing their shots."

"That happen often?"

"More than I'd like."

The barista called their names, and Robert excused himself to get their order. A man in a black suit and sunglasses sat at a neighboring table, taking a chair facing Sera. She shifted, her skin prickling like she was being stared at, but he bent his head over his phone. Robert returned, placing her steaming red eye in front of her before taking his seat.

"Hey, you didn't run away while I was gone. That's a good sign."

"You know I'm not the type to run."

"That I do."

"So, you in touch with anyone from the old unit? I haven't kept up, I'm afraid."

"Yeah, actually. You remember Mat? He lives in the city, too. Actually went and became a P.I."

"Ha, wild," said Sera. "He was always reading that ratty paperback."

"Trying to talk like Bogart."

"'Here's looking at you, kid.'"

Sera and Robert cracked up. Rocking back in her chair, tears forming in the corners of her eyes, Sera knocked over her drink. The steaming liquid splashed over the table and onto her dress. She shot to her feet. The coffee hadn't burned her—nothing ever burned her; it actually felt a little cool on her skin—but she was embarrassed.

"Are you okay?" asked Robert, also getting to his feet.

"Yeah, I'm fine," she said. "I'll be right back."

She quick-stepped past him deeper into the café, following the restroom signs. Once in the ladies' room she tried to sop up the spreading coffee stain with a fistful of paper towels, cursing herself for being such a klutz. Self-directed anger and a lack of sleep wasn't a good combination for her self control, so it wasn't a surprise when the paper towels caught on fire, but it was an inconvenience. She tossed the half-damp, half-burning wad into the sink and ran the tap, hoping the smoke wouldn't set off the fire alarm. At least her dress hadn't combusted.

Staring into her reflected eyes she said, "Get a hold of yourself, Lawson."

Once she thought she had herself back under control, and with the stain still damp but at least managed, she walked out of the restroom and right into the waiting stun gun of the man in the black suit. There was a sharp pain in her gut where he jabbed the prongs and her body seized up, limbs locked and stiff; she couldn't even open her mouth to shriek. She toppled, and the man in the black suit caught her with an arm around the small of her back.

"Easy, just relax," said the man as he dragged her towards a door labeled 'fire exit.'

A sharp crack sounded. The man in the black suit dropped Sera and fell to his knees. Robert stood over him, cane held up like a baseball bat. He gave the man in black another whack across the back.

Extending a hand to Sera he said, "On your feet, Lawson, we gotta move."

Her head was fuzzy, her vision swam and every inch of her body tingled with pins and needles. She tried to stand but her limbs wouldn't cooperate. All that came out of her mouth were malformed vowels.

"Federal agent," said the man in black, waving a badge too quickly to read as he stood. "You have no idea how dangerous that thing is, and you're interfering with an arrest."

"Assault and kidnapping isn't an arrest," said Robert.

"Well you assaulted a federal agent, smart guy. Back off or I'll take you down, too."

Sera put a hand on the nearby wall, using it as support as she rose from the floor. The agent pulled a gun from under his blazer.

"Stay where you are!"

Clinging to the wall, Sera stood. Robert stepped between her and the gun. The agent's finger tightened on the trigger.

Flames leapt from Sera in every direction. The gun melted in the agent's hand as his flesh vaporized off his bones. Fire leapt up the brick walls, liquefied the linoleum floor, assailed the plaster ceiling. Light bulbs burst in their fixtures, raining sparks and molten glass.

Once again Sera found herself standing naked in a public place, her clothes as much ash as the former man in black, but at least she wasn't alone this time. Robert, standing unharmed in the middle of the inferno, had undergone a transformation. In the light and heat of the flames scales of ruby and gold had materialized, covering him from head to foot. His prosthetic had burned and melted away, but a clawed, reptilian leg had grown to replace it.

He turned to her and said, "Well, I wasn't expecting that."

"You're not dead," she said, placing her palm on his pebbly chest, feeling the steady drum of his heart.

"Yeah, this is really a conversation I was hoping we could save until the second date" he said. "You look good, though."

Sera looked down at herself. Fire and smoke sheathed her body like a falcon's plumage. Wings of fire feathered out from behind her shoulders.

"I'm really glad I didn't kill you," she said, brain still too addled from the earlier electrocution and too enamored with Robert to really register the screams of terror and agony coming from the front of the café.

"We should get out of here," he said, stepping towards her.

"We should," she said, meeting him halfway.

Standing over the agent's crumbling bones, as the other patrons fled screaming, some with hair or clothes alight, and as the building burned down around them, Seraphina and Robert shared their first kiss. On wings of ruby scale and flame they rose into the air and blazed like colliding suns.

A Bond of Embers
Erin Casey

The world whisked past Lorelie's eyes as she soared on the back of a phoenix. She clung to Cassandra's waist with one arm as her girlfriend tugged gently on the reins. Cass's bonded phoenix, Tempest, angled her wings and tail, veering in the direction she was guided. The great blue bird trilled a note of satisfaction as warm thermals carried them higher into the sky. The breeze ruffled her azure feathers, barely making a sound. Had she been engulfed in flames, the wind would have ignited her fire and devoured anyone who wasn't already bonded with a phoenix.

Lorelie included.

"Are you sure about this?" Cass asked, not for the first time. Her girlfriend glanced back at her with warm, brown eyes. The sun kissed her dark skin and made her braided black hair glow. Lorelie couldn't hide a happy smile. She'd never get tired of looking at her beloved partner.

"Of course I'm not," Lorelie said. "But when has that ever stopped me?" She shifted carefully and leaned back enough to look at the small leather map pinned to Cass's vest. "Just past the crest of that mountain there, and through the ravine. That's where she'll be."

Tempest's body rumbled beneath her as the phoenix made a worried noise. "Is it wrong to hope the map has brought us to a dead end?"

Lorelie cracked a grin. "You aren't scared, are you, Tempest?"

The phoenix huffed and rolled a bright green eye back at her. "Have I ever shown fear in the face of battle?"

"Never," Cass said and ruffled the phoenix's feathers fondly. It earned her a pleased squawk. Cass's scritches turned to soothing pets. "But I wouldn't fault you if you were afraid now. We're not searching for any ordinary phoenix," she added, glancing at Lorelie. "It could get dangerous."

Lorelie kept quiet. Cass didn't need to tell her twice.

The kingdom of flames, their home, was devoted solely to phoenixes. At an early age, children and fledglings were brought together in a ritual and formed an everlasting bond. Children became immune to phoenix fire, and phoenixes could speak mentally to their human, as well as sense their emotions. They grew up together, rode on the wind as one, shared their meals, their beds, everything. Once they joined the army, the human counterparts were named Firetamers. Human and phoenix alike became family and protected each other from the other kingdoms who sought to snuff out their reign of fire.

The kingdom of wind and dragons thought her people were foolish to bond with phoenixes and treat them like equals. They expected their dragons to serve them with undying loyalty, and in return, they were given food and shelter. That alone should have sufficed. The dragons were treated as little more than pack mules, though if you suggested such a thing to a dragonrider, they'd call you blasphemous.

The magicians of the earth weren't much better with their forced familiars. They tethered their spells to beasts who served them with a twisted sense of love. Familiars laid down their lives in servitude to the magicians. And once a familiar died, the magician cast aside her peon and chose another.

Finally, the sirens of the water kingdom had the whole sea at their command. But they mostly kept to themselves unless the other warring nations polluted their waters and stole too many fish. Or if the sirens were in search of a fleshy meal. Phoenix. Dragon. Human. Familiar. It didn't matter to them. Flesh was flesh, and they sang their haunting songs to lure their prey in and fill their bellies.

I wonder if they have the same bitter feelings toward us, Lorelie thought to herself.

The kingdoms had been at war since well before she was born, each one vying to either be the true rulers of the world of Migara, or to protect what land they called home. For generations, her family had been great Firetamers. But, a great betrayal had severed her family's connection with the phoenixes. It was only by the grace of their queen that Lorelie had even been allowed to stay in the kingdom. It didn't make life easy for Lorelie, but she didn't care much about what others thought of her. She cared far more about righting the sins of her brethren.

Lorelie tightened her hold on her girlfriend, sensing her unease. "Hey, it's going to be fine."

"You don't know that," Cass said, her voice taking on a serious tone. "Lore, no one's been able to talk reason into her. And you can't handle the fire like I can. What if she loses her mind like the rumors whisper? What if she attacks you? What if—"

"What if I trip walking into the cave and impale myself on a pointy rock?" Lorelie interrupted with a strained smile. "What ifs aren't going to fix anything. Our numbers are dwindling as the dragon kingdom gets closer and closer to taking us out. We need all the help we can get. And besides, I owe it to her to try to make things right."

Cass sighed. "It's not your burden to bear. You didn't betray her."

"Doesn't matter," Lorelie said and pressed her head against Cassandra's back. "*My* family hurt her. So, I make it right." She took a deep, soothing breath and rolled her shoulders, loosening knots and tension. She rested her chin on Cass and held on tight as Tempest dove down through the ravine. A great waterfall poured into a glittering pool, the entire area surrounded by pine trees. Just at the edge of the lush green, a cave emerged. The entrance snarled at them with jagged teeth made of stalagmites and stalactites.

Tempest circled around the area twice before landing at the lip of the cave. Nothing except the wind howling softly in the distance greeted them. Lorelie stared into the darkness and swallowed a lump in her throat. "This is it."

She slid off Tempest's back and rested a hand against the phoenix's side. Cass hopped down beside her. Normally she would have loosened Tempest's saddle to give her a reprieve, but none of them knew what to expect. So a quick getaway was more than a little desirable.

Lorelie licked her dry lips. She took a step forward but didn't get far before Cassandra grabbed her hand.

"Wait," Cass said and pulled Lorelie into her arms, holding her tightly against her strong chest. "I love you, you stubborn woman," Cass said and kissed her forehead.

"You wouldn't have me any other way. And…I love you, too."

Offering one last smile to Cass and Tempest, Lorelie slipped through the jagged stone teeth and made her way toward her fate. The cave was eerily quiet save for the faint trickle of water falling from the ceiling into a crystalline pool below. Moss and cave plants grew around her, splashing the dark stone with splotches of emerald. While the entrance had been chilly, the deeper she walked, the warmer it felt. More plants grew, and golden and violet flowers poked their heads through rock crevices.

Lorelie shifted her goggles and rested them atop her short, red hair. She pulled off her cloak and laid it gently over a ledge as the heat grew too oppressive. Without it, her missing arm was exposed. A fake, wooden forearm and hand were buckled around her elbow. She rubbed her bicep, working out a few cramps and looked around as she stepped through another cave entrance.

Fire flickered in sconces on the wall. A thick rug covered in feathers lounged in front of a makeshift hearth. Stone shelves held trinkets, bottles, and books. A work table was covered in scrolls and a few items she didn't recognize. A keg of open mead rested beside it, filling Lorelie's nose with the scent of honey and yeast. Lorelie bypassed the drink and stepped toward the books instead. She brushed her fingers delicately over the pages.

"What are you doing here?" a voice boomed suddenly through the room.

Lorelie jumped back, causing the book to tumble to the floor. She spun around on her leather boots but couldn't find the source of the sound. With a grimace, she crouched and picked up the tome. "I'm sorry to disturb you. But I was hoping to have an audience with Nymora."

A snort greeted her request. "She's not interested in those who invade her home."

"Well, I wouldn't exactly say I invaded. More like, I invited myself in." Lorelie placed the book on the table and settled a hand on her hip. "My name is Lorelie. You wouldn't know me, but I think you'll recognize my family name."

"And why should it matter to me?"

Lorelie fought back the anxiety tightening her chest. "I'm of the Morwyn line."

Something moved so swiftly Lorelie didn't have a chance to actually see it before she was knocked off of her feet. She yelped as her back struck the floor, her hand moving to catch her head before it smacked against stone. The blade on her hip was yanked free and tossed to the side where it clattered across the ground.

Suddenly, a heavy foot fell on her chest and pinned her.

Lorelie blinked and stared up at the angry violet eyes staring down at her, encased in a golden-feathered face.

"Why would you dare come here, Morwyn traitor?" A vicious beak snapped inches from her nose.

Lorelie struggled to suck in the breath both the ground and paw had stolen from her. "To make amends," she said and reached up to touch the phoenix's foot. The phoenix glowered and dug her talons into Lorelie's shirt, giving her pause. "I've heard rumors of what my great grandfather did to you. I've come to apologize and ask for your forgiveness."

Nymora leaned down and hissed in Lorelie's face. "Nothing you say or do can make up for the atrocities that traitor committed."

"Then help me understand what he did so I don't make the same mistake," Lorelie pleaded. "I want to hear *your* story, Nymora."

"Ha! So you can betray me, too?"

"No!" Lorelie cried. She squeezed Nymora's toe, grimacing as the talons poked through her tunic and pricked her skin. "I want to fix this. And if that means serving you and being your prisoner, I'll do it."

Nymora snapped her black beak tightly together. After a long moment, she leaned her head close to Lorelie's and tilted it so her violet eye could take her in in full. "Why would you believe me? No other Morwyn has."

"Try me," Lorelie said. She met Nymora's judging gaze, unblinking. "I may bear his name, but I'm not Baska Morwyn."

"We will see." Nymora pulled back and settled down on her haunches. She ruffled her mighty golden wings along her back and watched as Lorelie slowly sat up. "What have you heard?"

Oh, yeah, this is going to go over well, Lorelie thought bitterly as she folded her legs beneath her. She sat in front of the phoenix, staying low and less threatening. Her gaze briefly crept over to her sword, but a faint hiss from Nymora jerked her attention back to the mighty phoenix. "You and my great grandfather, Baska, bonded when you were both young. Your bond was legendary, like you shared one mind. You...you both were revered. And when he became a Firetamer, and you both joined the army, he was a fierce, dangerous warrior, especially with you at his side."

Nymora preened one of her wings lightly. "Go on."

Lorelie rubbed her shoulder and tilted her head back. "He wanted to lead an attack against the dragon kingdom. And you refused. You two argued and fought about it until he attacked you. You broke the bond with him, something that's never been done before. And it put a curse on my family so that none of us can bond with phoenixes." She looked at Nymora. "Do I have it right?"

Nymora scoffed. "Your story would paint me as the villain, as the coward who didn't want to protect our kingdom from the dragons."

Lorelie quickly shook her head. "I don't see it like that. You must have had a good reason to refuse him, right? Why? What did he want you to do?"

To Lorelie's surprise, Nymora didn't snap at her or knock her to the floor again. Instead, the phoenix turned away and walked toward the hearth. Fire flickered on her feathers and jumped onto the dying embers, reigniting them in a golden glow. She plucked a feather free and reached for a bottle resting beside the flames. "It's better if I show you."

In a swift motion, she tossed the feather and bottle into the roaring fire. They exploded in a cloud of blinding golden smoke, sending Lorelie rolling across the ground. She coughed and blinked through the haze. Only, she didn't find herself in the middle of Nymora's cave anymore. Instead, she sat on a castle's parapets with the sunset blazing in the horizon.

"Wh-where am I?" Lorelie stuttered.

She was answered by a mighty screech. Lorelie looked up in alarm as a phoenix descended from the sky, an armored rider upon her back. Lorelie rolled out of the way just in time for the bird to land. The phoenix waited patiently as her rider dismounted then folded her wings at her side. When she lifted her head, Lorelie's mouth dropped.

It was Nymora, only, a much younger version. The phoenix turned her sharp eyes to her rider as he pulled off his helmet. A long frosted brown braid fell down his back. His face was younger than Lorelie remembered from paintings, but the scar over her right eye revealed his identity.

"Grandfather Baska?" she asked in wonder. She pushed herself to her feet and walked toward him. How was this possible? He'd died years ago! Biting her lip, she reached for his arm.

Her fingers went through him like a ghost as he faced Nymora.

"It's nearly time," he said in a deep baritone. "Their warriors will have drunken themselves into a stupor after the solstice celebration. It's the perfect time to attack."

Nymora made a rumbled noise in her throat and glanced toward the dragon kingdom. "We may be able to defeat their warriors, but the citizens could still stand against us."

"That's why we're not just targeting their warriors," Baska replied. He grinned fiercely at Nymora. "We'll take them all down at once. Man. Woman. Child. None of them will haunt our gates again."

Lorelie's mouth dropped open in horror. *Children?* He wanted to murder *children?*

"What?" Nymora hissed. "You said nothing of this to me! Killing their mightiest I understand, but babes?"

"Those children will grow to be warriors and will try to avenge their parents!" Baska argued. "We don't have to kill them all. We'll take some as hostages, so the survivors won't dare come after us. The families will all be sheltered in the barracks. It'll be nothing for you to set them aflame. The few that escape, our Flametamers will snatch up."

Nymora drew her head back in disgust. "How dare you ask this of me? This isn't right. This is murder!"

"This is war!" Baska roared in her face. "Or have you forgotten the many Flametamers and phoenixes who have died at their hands and their dragons' teeth?" He planted his hands against the stone wall and grinned. "After tonight, no one else has to die. We'll end the war."

"No," Nymora growled.

Baska looked at her and narrowed his eyes. "*No?*"

"I won't do this," the phoenix said, shaking her head. "I can't. You ask too much of me, Baska. I would follow you to the end of time, but I won't do this."

Baska glowered into her eyes. But there was something else there: hurt, disbelief, betrayal…a glint of madness. He pushed away from the wall and approached her, one hand on his sword. "You've been my loyal companion for decades, but now, when I need you the most, you decide to betray me?"

"No! But I will not give into your madness! Can't you see your lust for success and dominance is blinding you to needless suffering? Even if we did succeed, their remaining warriors would avenge their loved ones."

"Then we burn them all!" He drew his sword and thrust it into the air. "Fight beside me, Nymora. Don't force my hand against you."

Nymora spread her legs and crouched low, her violet eyes misting. "I won't fight you, Baska. You're my friend, my partner."

Baska wavered for a moment. But as the sun set and the last dying flames flickered in the reflection of his sword, his face darkened. With a roar, he threw himself upon Nymora.

"No!" Lorelie cried and tried to get between them, but Baska passed through her.

Nymora staggered away, lifting her wing to defend herself. The sword sliced through it, sending blood arcing through the air.

All at once, the image fell in a cloud of golden dust. Lorelie found herself on her knees, tears running down her cheeks. She stared at her hand, imagining it stained in blood, just like Baska's. "How could he do that to you?" She sniffed and looked over at Nymora.

The great phoenix lifted her wing. A jagged scar lined her flesh from top to bottom. It was a wonder Nymora's wing was still attached.

Lorelie's stomach lurched in disgust. She'd known he'd attacked Nymora, but not how. And to learn the truth behind *why* he'd hurt his partner left an acidic taste in her mouth. Of all the ways he could have betrayed her. No wonder Nymora had broken the bond! Who would want to be tethered to someone willing to kill babes in their beds?

Slowly, Lorelie bowed her head. "There are no words that can undo the damage done to you. And I know there's nothing I can say to make you trust me. But...I'm sorry. I'm so sorry he hurt you. He was wrong. And I understand now why you broke the bond."

The phoenix was quiet. Lorelie kept her head down, but she felt Nymora staring at her, judging her. And for a moment, she feared the phoenix would take revenge on her.

Could I fault her if she did? she wondered. *She didn't deserve this.*

"What happened to your arm?" Nymora asked.

The question startled Lorelie. She glanced at her missing limb. "A Firetamer and her phoenix were knocked from the sky and attacked by a dragonrider. I tried to fight them off with my sword, but the dragon was stronger. When the dragon spit his deadly fire at them, I got in the way at the same time the phoenix attacked. Both of their flames incinerated my arm. But at least it stopped the dragon from killing the phoenix and her companion."

"You fought knowing you could die since you didn't have protection from phoenix or dragon fire," Nymora said quietly. She ground her beak and looked away. "Reckless. Stubborn."

Lorelie chuckled. "I've been called all these things before. And worse."

"You have Morwyn blood in you, that's for certain."

Lorelie winced and looked down. "I'm not like him."

"Yes, you are," Nymora argued. Before Lorelie could defend herself, the phoenix stretched out her golden wing and settled it on Lorelie's back. "But you're the good part of him. He was a mighty warrior, but he would have never risked his life like that. He would have used the Firetamer and the phoenix as a distraction to take the dragon from behind and possibly would have lost them both. You demonstrated true bravery. Heh, you even tried to step between me and Baska when you knew they were just memories." She squinted. "Unless you're a storyteller like he was, and your words are full of lies."

Lorelie couldn't stop herself from laughing. She brushed tears from her eyes. "Oh, I can't lie to save my life. You can ask my girlfriend, Cass, and she'll tell you the same thing. I got in trouble a lot as a child because I could never fib about my wrongdoings. Couldn't keep secrets either, so I ruined many a surprise party."

Nymora lifted her head, amused. "Then answer me this. Did you only come to make amends?"

"No," Lorelie said. She ran her hand along her short red hair in hesitation. "I had hoped you would lift the curse on my line, too, so I could help fight properly. I'm older, but maybe another phoenix will still take me on as a Firetamer." She bit her lip and met Nymora's violet eyes. "Maybe...you would take me as your partner?"

The phoenix snorted and withdrew her wing. She stepped away from Lorelie, taking with her her warmth and comfort. "So you wish to use me."

"Not use you. Work beside you." Lorelie pushed herself to her feet. "You were one of the strongest, bravest phoenixes there ever was. If you don't want to partner with me, I understand. But please, come back. Baska did you wrong, but the kingdom still adores you and needs you. I'm begging you, Nymora. Not for my sake, but for the sake of the kingdom and her people."

She held out her wooden hand imploringly.

Nymora paused near the hearth and gazed into the fiery depths. Silence settled between them, sending doubt and fear twisting through Lorelie's stomach.

The phoenix finally looked back, her gaze settling on the wooden arm. "You're the first of your family to come seek me out to make amends. The rest only wanted the curse lifted. Others have been Firetamers and phoenixes begging me to join the fray. There's a part of me that's weary of fighting, which is partially why I left. And yet, there's another that burns for it. But only with the *right* companion."

The dismissive tone made Lorelie's shoulders drop. Well, it had been a long shot. "I understand. There are some Firetamers who lost their partners and need a new one. Strong, trustworthy warriors."

"But I don't want one of *them*," Nymora said and stepped closer. "I don't know their hearts. I haven't seen their sacrifice. But I feel I know yours. And I know what you've given." She brushed her wounded wing against Lorelie's wooden arm.

Hope fluttered in Lorelie's stomach. "I...you mean...you'll bond with me?"

Nymora cocked her head. "Yes...but with a price." She laid a talon on Lorelie's shoulder and peered hard into her eyes. "I will invoke the bond, but with a change. Any injury, any pain I endure, you will feel as well. Maybe that will make you think twice about betraying me, too. Do you agree?"

Lorelie stared at the talon. She'd never heard of that sort of bond before. To accept it could mean pain and death if Nymora ever fell. The alternative was to never bond with a phoenix, especially not Nymora. She swallowed hard. "I accept."

Nymora's body suddenly glistened as gold and violet fire rushed through her feathers. Her wings ignited and the tufts on her head hissed to life with flames. "Do you know the bonding ritual?"

Lorelie nodded and reached for the straps on her arm. She put her arm on the table, so as not to make it extra kindling, and stood before Nymora in only her tunic and pants. "I trust you, Nymora."

The phoenix stretched her wings up and created a circle of fire around them. "Step into the flames, Lorelie."

Lorelie curled her fingers into a fist, her heart pounding in her chest. Beads of sweat rolled down her face as she stared at the mesmerizing flames. If she didn't trust the phoenix, or herself, she'd go up in smoke.

This could all be a trap and her attempt to get revenge, a negative voice whispered in her ear.

No, Lorelie countered. *I said I trusted her, and damn it, I mean it.*

With clenched jaw and hand, she stepped into the fire.

Heat rushed across her body, nearly stealing the breath from her lungs. Fire flowed around, caressing her flesh and clothing. Fabric sizzled and her fingers ached from the burn. For a moment, she waited for the engulfing flames to devour her. That's what everyone expected. But she shoved the doubt away and took another step into the inferno. It washed over her, through her, crawled along her arms and twisted into her hair. A tendril brushed her lips until she parted them. Suddenly, the fire flowed into her mouth and filled her veins, igniting them almost as much as Cass's kiss. She drank it in and felt her throat burn.

Suddenly, the fire dispersed. Lorelie collapsed from the sudden shock, directly into Nymora's soft breast feathers. The phoenix draped her wings around Lorelie's body and steadied her. Lorelie panted and leaned her head against Nymora's chest. As her heart pounded, she heard Nymora's heart beat to the same tempo.

A tear trickled down Lorelie's cheek. "I can feel it. The bond."

"As do I," Nymora said softly. The phoenix brushed her beak through Lorelie's hair and preened it sweetly. "I truly see you now. Your mind. Your heart. You spoke the truth."

"Heh, I told you I couldn't lie." Lorelie ran her fingers along Nymora's beautiful feathers. "I can feel your pain and grief," she murmured. "But hope's ignited too. I'd like to think I might be the cause of that."

Nymora chuckled deeply. "A bit haughty, too, aren't you?" She looked around her cave. "It will be strange to come out of isolation. It's been so long since I last saw my brethren."

"They miss you," Lorelie said. She pushed herself upright and fixed a few of the disheveled feathers. "You don't have to be alone anymore. Not so long as you're stuck with me."

Nymora bent down beside Lorelie and cocked her head. "Then you'd best hop on if we're going to make it home."

Lorelie hesitated as she stared at Nymora's bare back. "Won't I need a saddle?"

"Do you trust me not to drop you?"

"I trusted you not to turn me into a pile of ash, so, yes?" Lorelie gripped one of Nymora's wings and pulled herself up onto the phoenix's back, with a little help from her partner. Partner…what a strange notion. She tightened her legs around Nymora and leaned forward, dazzled by the height. Tempest was a big phoenix, but Nymora? Lorelie didn't think she'd seen any phoenix quite so large.

As Nymora stepped around the table, Lorelie snagged her wooden arm and started to rebuckle it. Nymora moved with ease beneath her, her body swaying, but in a comfortable way that didn't threaten to send Lorelie flying into a wall. She fetched Lorelie's fallen sword and offered it back. As she did, the tip nicked Nymora's toe. Lorelie winced, feeling pain in her finger. Blood blossomed on the tip, reminding her of the promise she'd made. Pain for pain.

As they slipped into the next cave, Lorelie retrieved her cloak and wrapped it around herself.

Tempest's blue glow beckoned them toward the entrance. The moment Tempest and Cass spotted them, Cass gasped and nearly burst into tears of relief.

Lorelie waved cheerfully. "I told you she wouldn't roast me!"

"My lady," Tempest said and bowed her head regally.

Nymora bumped her beak against the other phoenix's. "Enough of that. Just call me Nymora."

Tempest smiled and ruffled her wings excitedly against Cass's legs. Cass touched her neck and reached out toward Lorelie. As Lorelie leaned down, Cassandra kissed her deeply.

"Don't scare me like that again," Cass said, poking Lorelie in the cheek.

"Eh, you know it's not the last time. But I'll try." Lorelie winked and looked off the mountain's edge and into the distance. She slid her goggles over her eyes. "Are you ready, Nymora?"

In answer, the phoenix shrieked into the sky and leapt off the ledge. Fire blazed across her body and Lorelie's. Only this time, there was no pain or uncertainty. She felt nothing but warmth.

Lorelie smiled, giddy. It was suddenly becoming very real to her what had just happened. No longer would she be the lone warrior without a phoenix. No longer would she have to endure the glares and snickers from people who shunned her for the curse on her family and the sins of Baska. Instead, she'd finally become what she'd always dreamed of: a Firetamer.

Even better, with Nymora at her side, she'd never be alone.

FIREARM
Theodore Michelet Sterling

ONE: Bone to Pick

Woggle, the axe-throwing orc, sat wrapped in a sheet on an exam table. Dr. Hogger, orc physician, auscultated, palpated, and stared at the patient's various bits (through unnervingly dark tinted goggles). As he did, the doctor placed his personal stamp on sections of a parchment he held on a clipboard.

Woggle snickered. "Give it to me straight, doc. Will I live?"

"Cute, but yes—until you face the Rogue Drow."

"So I'm in?"

Dr. Hogger snickered back. "About that..."

The exam room door burst open. A short orc entered. "Are you done yet?"

"Almost, Fepig," said the doctor.

The little orc hopped up and pulled the doctor's clipboard to his eye level. He ran his finger down the parchment. "Yes, yes, looks good. Woggle will be an excellent addition to our gladiatorial troupe—Wait." Fepig squinted. "You haven't placed the final stamp."

"But—"

"Just stamp it so I can file the report. Woggle needs to meet with his team at lunch."

Dr. Hogger glanced from Woggle to Fepig. "Right."

He placed the final stamp.

Fepig snatched the form.

"What's the team's name?" asked Woggle.

"I'm so glad you asked." Fepig cleared his throat. "Messenger."

Messenger? "Huh," said Woggle. "Why Messenger?"

Fepig's pointy ears perked up. "Why, to send the message: 'We orcs of the Northern Territory are a force to be reckoned with, and—'"

"Yes, yes, off you go." Dr. Hogger hustled Fepig out of the exam room.

"But—"

"File the form. Tell the general it's all taken care of." He shut the door. "Where were we?"

Woggle wiggled off the exam table and shivered as his feet touched the cold stone floor. "Getting dressed." He reached for his clothes pile.

"Yes, but—," Dr. Hogger bared his crooked teeth, "—there is still the matter of payment."

Woggle scoffed. "Payment? This is your job."

"And my patients enjoy showing their appreciation with a small...bit of something."

Woggle clutched the clothes wad to his chest. "How about a bit of advice? Stop asking."

"Confound it! I expected not requesting a tip would have avoided such a witty retort."

"Hmm." Woggle affected a nasally drone. "'Where's My tip?'"—in a lower register—"'Here's a tip....'" His voice normalized. "Yeah, I can see that." Woggle cleared his throat. "So, here's a tip: Work on your delivery." He unraveled his crimson uniform.

A long, slender bone fell out and clattered on the stone floor.

A silvery luster coated its surface.

Crap.

Dr. Hogger gazed at it (through those impenetrable goggles).

Woggle snapped it up and struggled into his uniform.

His elbow jammed in his sleeve.

"Quite a nice specimen," said Dr. Hogger, in a hushed, sing-song manner.

Woggle pulled at the hem, but the fabric clung to his now sweaty green body. "Yup, found it this morning."

"Where?"

"The boneyard."

"Of course."

"You're free to search there for one just like it."

Dr. Hogger's face blanked. In a mechanical monotone, he stated, "I want that one."

How did he become so creepy, so quickly? "You know what?" Woggle hopped to a pair of bags by the door while forcing his legs through his trousers. "I bet I've got a 'bit of something' in—," he lifted a bag, "—one of my axe sacks." He reached inside it.

"Axe sacks." (The monotone intensified.)

Woggle handed Dr. Hogger a throwing axe.

The doctor brushed it aside. "The bone. Give it to me."

Woggle cringed, but...how did this doctor orc—not a real, fightin' orc—think he could intimidate him? Axe-throwing champion. Member of the elite gladiatorial troupe Messenger (Messenger, really?). Keeper of the awesome bone he found this morning.

Woggle straightened his back. "Well, you can't have it. In fact, you can't have this, either." He returned the axe to the bag.

Dr. Hogger's jaw tightened. "You are making a grave mistake."

"The only mistake I made was lingering here after Fepig swiped your form." He stomped his feet into his boots and opened the door. "Now, if you'll excuse me, I have a luncheon to attend."

He exited and shivered again (but not from the chilly floor).

He should have zinged him with another quip about tips.

Fepig escorted Woggle to a table set on a stage in the mess hall. Three muscled orcs, his fellow Messengers, waited for him. (But if they were each a Messenger, shouldn't their team be Messengers?)

"Why are we eating on a stage?" asked Woggle.

"So everyone can watch you." Fepig waved to the sea of orcs sitting at long tables in the rest of the mess hall, munching away.

"Heh, how about that?"

Fepig pointed to each Messenger: "Fargar, the hammer orc, Guppig, the ball-and-chain orc, and Eckle, the weight-throwing orc, this is Woggle, the, uh—what's your gimmick?"

"Gimmick?"

"Every gladiator must have his own gimmick. What's yours again?"

"I guess it's axe-throwing."

"Hmm, an axe-thrower. Eckle, how about we call yours weight-*tossing*—"

"Throw, not toss," said Eckle.

"Two throwers?" Fepig shook his head. "How can this team compete against the Rogue Drow?"

"Two brawlers, two ranged attackers," said Fargar. "It'll be fine."

"You four won the trials," said Fepig. "Far be it for me to question the team's balance."

"Grub, now," said Guppig.

"On the way." Fepig left.

"So," said Woggle, "just saw the doctor. He wanted a tip."

"Tell me about it," said Fargar.

"How much you pay him?" asked Eckle.

Woggle smirked. "Nothing."

The three stared at him.

Woggle furrowed his brow. "What?"

A greasy orc in a crumpled, stained chef's hat approached the table. "What can I get for you fellas?"

They ignored him.

The orc chef clicked his tongue. "How about I come back later?" He fled.

"How—," Fargar stammered, "—how d'you get the final stamp without paying him?"

"Oh," said Woggle, "Fepig made him stamp it before he asked for a 'bit of something.' So, I said, 'Here's a bit of advice: Drop the creepy goggles.'"

Eckel's jaw hung loose. "You—you said that?"

"Yup," said Woggle, had he thought of it at the time.

"Fool," grumbled Guppig. "Where's that chef?"

"Come on," said Woggle. "What's the worst—?"

"You!" shouted a familiar voice.

Shivers ran up Woggle's spine.

Everyone turned to the mess hall entrance.

Dr. Hogger pointed, scowling.

Diners lurched aside as Hogger marched to Messenger's table. He placed his arms behind his back and leaned toward Woggle. "You know what I want."

Fargar, Eckel, and Guppig scooted farther away.

Woggle stood and faced his fellow Messengers. "You won all those trials. Why are you afraid of this guy?"

They studied the notches and woodgrain of the table.

Woggle turned to Dr. Hogger. "Well, I'm not afraid of you." He held out the bone. "You want this?"

Its luster drew the gaze of everyone in the hall.

He clutched it to his chest. "You can have it—when you pry it from my cold, dead fingers."

Dr. Hogger shrugged. "So be it."

He struck Woggle in the shoulder with a bonesaw, and ripped it back, severing muscle, tendon, bone, and more muscle.

Woggle watched blood gush onto the floor. "Oh, that's why."

He slumped into the puddle with a splat.

TWO: Life-Saving Measures

Woggle blinked his eyes.

He lay on Dr. Hogger's examination table. Thick blood-stained bandages clung to where his arm used to be.

His axe-throwing arm.

He shot up to a sitting position, but pain pulsed through his wound, and his head spun.

"Easy, easy," said Dr. Hogger, while guiding him to a resting position.

"What.... what...?"

"Relax." Dr. Hogger beamed and held the bone before Woggle's eyes. "I cannot thank you enough for this magnificent bone. Why, it must count as payment for both the examination and saving your life. Just now."

Woggle sat up again and squinted. "Saved—?"

"Shh." Hogger eased him back down. "No need to thank me. This bone is payment enough."

"My arm. You took my bloody arm."

"And bloody it was."

"Can you—," Woggle suppressed a sob, "—put it back on?"

"Oh, no. Your fingers were cold and dead, the exact conditions under which you gifted me this wonderful bone."

"I said that, didn't I?" He didn't bother suppressing the next sob. "I can't be a Messenger like this."

"Don't worry!"

"Really? I could still join the team?"

Hogger laughed. "Of course not! Listen to yourself."

"You said not to worry."

"Yes, don't worry about the team. They already found a replacement."

"Who?"

Hogger grinned and thumbed toward himself. "Me!"

"You? Why you?"

"I must have impressed them with my impromptu amputation skills."

"What'll I do now?"

"First, you must tend to your wound." Dr. Hogger assisted Woggle to a sitting position and handed him a parchment covered in tiny stamps. "Follow these instructions, and you'll be fine in no time."

"Fine? Without an arm?" Woggle gritted his teeth. "My axe-throwing arm?"

"You'd be surprised." Hogger pointed to the bottom of the page. "Check these guys out."

Woggle sat in one of many stools arranged in a circle—except for a gap near the room's entrance. More orcs took seats around him. One missing a foot entered on crutches. Another bore a hook for a hand. A third wore an eyepatch.

He would have traded places with any of them, even the hook-handed orc. At least he had some arm left. How could so much misfortune befall him?

A persistent squeak grew louder from the outside.

In rolled a wheelchair, which slowed to a stop in the circle's gap. Its owner's limbs—arms and legs—ended at barely a foot long, each.

The limbless orc surveyed the group. "Everyone's here? Let's begin. You can call me Stubbins."

Woggle winced. "Oof, sorry about the nickname."

The others stared at him.

"What?"

"It's my real name," said Stubbins.

"Your name was Stubbins, even before—"

"A dragon bit off my arms and legs? Yes."

"A dragon?"

"There he goes," muttered the eyepatch wearer.

Stubbins recounted how he had captured and tamed the first dragon mount for the Northern Territory leader. But Stubbins' mission to capture the second went... poorly.

"He spat my legs out. Must a thought my arms would a tasted better. Showed him."

Crutches, Hook, and Eyepatch seemed bored (how many times had they heard this story?), but Woggle leaned in. "How? How could you move on from that?"

Stubbins grinned. "When there's so much to do, how couldn't I?"

Woggle stood up. "To do? Look at you. You can't do anything. None of us can!"

"Here we go," muttered Eyepatch.

"What's that?"

Hook raised his hook. "Stubbins tells his dragon story, the new guy freaks out and rants about being useless."

"We've seen it all before," said Crutches.

"Useless! That's the word," said Woggle. "Why keep us around? They should just throw us into the boneyard and... and...."

Woggle swayed. Two Stubbins sat where one had before. Two Eyepatches, two Hooks, and two Crutches (with his four, uh, crutches). He rubbed his face. "What's going—? Not again."

He slumped to the floor.

THREE: Divine Intervention

Squeaking.

Woggle sat in Stubbins' wheelchair. It squeaked away as he zoomed down the hall.

Sweat covered his body, but he shivered. His head pounded (from the squeaking?). "What's going...?"

"You're festering," said Dr. Hogger's voice from behind the wheelchair. "Tell me, when did you last change your wound dressing?"

"Changed? I haven't changed it yet."

"You've been wearing the same dressing for four days?"

"The sheet you gave me said...." Woggle caught his breath. "Said change it weekly."

"Oops. My bad. Supposed to say daily."

Great. Woggle was going to die of a stamp-o. "Where are we going?"

"A festering wound like this, I'd chop off, but you got nothing left to chop."

"You can't help me?"

"No, but someone else might."

"Who?"

"She allows me five referrals a year. Lucky you. You're my fifth."

She? Female orcs didn't exist. "Are you taking me to see Hete, oh God of War, may she reign...." He couldn't finish his thought.

"Not quite."

Dr. Hogger stopped before dragon-embossed double doors. Two large orc guards stood by.

One lowered a spear. "She's busy. Leave."

Dr. Hogger handed him a small card. "Number five."

The guard waved them in.

A young human woman in flowing white diaphanous fabric levitated over an ornate rug, legs crossed, eyes closed, and fingers and thumbs formed in circles.

Woggle squinted. "The oracle?" He craned his neck around the wheelchair to look at Hogger. "Why—?"

Dr. Hogger sped away down the hall.

The guard shut the door.

"Doctor! Wait!"

Woggle's legs quaked, and he eased into the chair.

The oracle stood inches from him.

He recoiled, but she sniffed around him. And grimaced.

She rose into the air and waved her arms around.

Like blood-red snakes, bandages unraveled and floated to a corner by a golden spittoon.

Rotten meat aroma assaulted his olfactory system.

He leaned sideways and heaved. "Oh, Hete, why didn't I change it daily?"

The oracle curled her fingers like claws and raised her hands.

A phantom grip squeezed Woggle's ribs and crept toward the wound. Sharp, searing pain streaked through his body.

A stream of pus spewed from the wound into the spittoon.

The pressure released. His head swam, but somehow...he felt better, as if some foul disease had been squeezed from his body (which was basically what happened).

Woggle breathed slowly. "Thank you. I—"

The oracle stared at him, but waved at the spittoon.

Flames engulfed it, then died down, leaving ash and molten brass.

Smokiness displaced most of the rotten meat smell, but some still lingered. "Um...."

The oracle hovered toward a screen door cabinet and opened it.

Maggots swarmed over a hunk of rotten meat inside.

"Um...."

She swiped a double handful of squirmy things.

Oh, no.

She jammed them into his wound.

He cringed. "Why? Why?"

She hovered away and held her hands out, wiggling her fingers.

Her nails glowed green, as did the maggots.

The tiny worm-like grubs dug into the festering wound at double, triple, quadruple speed. Ticklish tingling spread through his wound, but changed into a satisfying sensation, like pulling off dead skin (which was basically what happened).

The maggots erupted from the wound as glowing adult flies. They buzzed at insane speed, then dropped dead (like flies). Their glowing faded, and the oracle lowered her hands.

Woggle inspected the wound as best he could.

No stink. No festering flesh. Just pink-red exposed muscle, like a raw steak.

"Um...."

The oracle took a deep breath and exhaled slowly. She clenched her fists and gritted her teeth.

The ragged edges of his skin inched across the open wound.

"Are you—," Woggle gulped, "—are you growing my arm back?"

She ignored him and continued to strain.

The skin edges met and formed a jagged scar.

She released her hands and sank to the floor.

"That's it?" Woggle got out of the wheelchair. "I'm back to where I was before I fainted. Armless. Useless."

She glanced at the arm he still had.

"Okay, not armless, but still useless. Why bother? You should have —"

She leaned closer.

"You should have let me die."

She shook her head and returned to her meditation pose over the ornate rug.

"Fine, go back to communing with Hete. Meanwhile, I'll wander the halls, shunned and forgotten." He clenched his (one) fist. "That Dr. Hogger. If I had my arm, I'd strangle that—that—" Woggle glanced at the oracle.

She remained in her pose, eyes closed, but in one hand she held out a small card.

He took it.

The card displayed three stamps: a scowling oracle, and two quarter moons.

"Return in two months?"

* * *

Over the next two months, Woggle attended the group. He learned Crutches's, Hook's, and Eyepatch's real names (Vitig, Throkka, and Umpi, if you must know). Stubbins introduced him to a secret gym they built in the boneyard.

"Funny you thought they should send us here to die," Stubbins had said, "'cause we come here to live."

And the group leader showed his independence, thanks in part to devices he created, comprising cones that fit over his limb stumps, with tools carved from bone attached. Grippers to grip his wheels; grabbers to grab; stilts to "walk" (short distances).

Woggle also learned Messenger had made their debut. And they beat the legendary undefeated Rogue Drow, a gladiatorial troupe of, well, rogue drow. However, the lead drow was missing, and the troll queen interfered... so, a victory with an asterisk*.

Still, a victory—without him.

Woggle flung a throwing axe.

Its head embedded into the giant shoulder blade they had propped up for target practice.

"Progress," said Stubbins.

"I was aiming for the other one." Woggle readied another axe. "Where do you think it came from?"

"Troll, probably. All orc kin come here to die, including the ogres and trolls."

"But not goblins."

"Bah, who knows about them?"

Woggle tossed it.

The second axe stuck next to the first.

"Accuracy's improving," said Stubbins.

"I was still aiming for the other one."

"Here. Let me give you a hand."

"Ha, ha. Hilarious."

"I mean it." Stubbins attached a grabber and lifted a skeletal ogre arm. Stringy ligaments still held it together. "Literally."

"What am I supposed to do with it?"

"Strap it on."

---

* Although orc stamps bear little resemblance to the written word, they do use an asterisk-like tiny star to indicate supplemental information.

* * *

"Are you trying to re-fester my wound? And it's huge."

"But just bones. It'll weigh about the same as an orc arm in the flesh."

"Seriously?" Woggle shook his head and strapped it in place.

He launched a third axe.

It thunked between the first two.

"Still can't hit the other shoulder blade," said Stubbins.

"No. I aimed between the axes."

"See? You just needed better balance."

"Balance. I'm getting better, but I'm nowhere near as good as before."

"Maybe you'll never battle the Rogue Drow, but you're at soldier level, at least."

The three neighboring axe heads blurred together in the dimming light, like a solid hunk of metal.

Woggle glanced at the sky.

Quarter moon.

"It's been two months—I have to go!"

Woggle found the oracle, but a thick apron and gloves covered her diaphanous clothing. "What's all that?"

With long tongs, she removed a crucible from a mini-forge, and poured molten metal into a mold.

She turned over a small hour glass and folded her arms.

"You couldn't have done this part during the two months?" asked Woggle.

The sand ran out. She split open the mold.

A dome-like shoulder guard fell out, embossed with ornate dragon-shaped patterns.

She tossed the ogre bones off Woggle's armless shoulder and strapped on the armor.

It weighed about the same as skeletal remains. "Better balance, but what are these?" He pointed to finger-like prongs along its surface.

The oracle hovered to a bench and donned a jeweler's loupe. She examined a large green rock. She wiggled her fingers.

Slashes of light sliced off fragments until the rock became a plate-sized emerald.

A rotten meat maggot farm, a mini-forge, a jeweler's bench—who knew an oracle needed so much equipment?

She levitated the giant gem to Woggle's shoulder plate and clutched her fingers.

The prongs clasped the emerald and held it in place.

Woggle whistled. "Pretty, but—"

She motioned for him to follow her.

The oracle led Woggle deep under the Northern Territory's mountain stronghold. They came to a stop in a vast chamber lit by an endless pool of magma.

Woggle's sweat evaporated as fast as it formed. "Phew. Hot enough for you?"

The oracle ignored him and dragged him up stone stairs carved from a massive stalagmite that ended with a platform extending over the pool.

"Um...."

The oracle spun around and sauntered to the edge.

With a wave, she cannonballed into the magma.

"Oracle, no! Wait, is that really your name?" Woggle glanced over the platform edge.

Only bubbles rose where she splashed down.

"Oh, oracle, why'd you do that?" She must have survived. She wouldn't sacrifice herself for a one-armed orc, would she?

The bubbles quickened, and a spout of magma rose above the platform.

Woggle backed away, but the spout lowered like a tentacle. Ripples flowed over it and sculpted its shape.

Snout, fangs, horns, and two glowing eyes.

A giant dragon. Made of magma.

"Hete!" Woggle kneeled. "Oh, God of War, long may you reign."

The magma dragon head snaked toward him. Her voice rattled the cavern. "Well?"

"The oracle. She sacrificed herself so I may see you. In the flesh— uh—lava—"

"Magma!"

"Right, magma. But I don't know why...."

A trail of small bubbles slid along the magma-dragon's body, up her neck, and stopped at her cheek.

The oracle's head and shoulders popped out and whispered in

Hete's ear (or pantomimed whispering; she made no sound).

Woggle covered his mouth (with the hand he still owned). "Oracle...?"

The oracle winked at Woggle, and sunk back into Hete's cheek. Bubbles reemerged and slunk down the magma-neck into the pool below.

Hete snickered. "I apologize. I should have anticipated your feeble orc mind would buckle in my immense presence."

"Um, thank you?"

"Your oracle has enlightened me with your tale of woe and vengeance."

"Vengeance?"

"Do you not seek revenge against the one who wronged you?"

Woggle scowled. "Dr. Hogger." He tilted his head. "Why do you care?"

"Vengeance quests bring me great satisfaction."

"But you're the god of war."

"Vengeance is a subcategory. Now, genuflect before me."

He glanced down. "Aren't I already?"

"No, you are kneeling. Raise one leg so your foot is on the ground, and keep the other knee...."

"Like this?"

"Correct." Her eyes widened, brightening the chamber. "Prepare to receive my blessing."

The over-sized emerald on his shoulder glowed with blinding intensity.

Woggle turned away, but it burned. His arm burned. His arm—his arm?

He dared to look.

His arm—he could feel it—composed of fire extended from the gem's surface.

He waved around his flaming hand. Tears formed in his eyes (but evaporated). "It's beautiful."

He extended it.

A stream of fire 30 feet long blasted from his palm.

Hete grinned. "Seek vengeance."

Woggle clenched his fiery fist. "I just want my bone back."

FOUR: Rebranding

Woggle kicked open the doors to the Northern Territory's mess hall, and pointed an accusing/flaming finger at Dr. Hogger, seated among the other Messengers at the staged table. "You!"

The physician froze mid-bite into a meaty drumstick.

Woggle marched toward him, finger still pointing/accusing/ flaming, and hopped onto the stage.

Dr. Hogger scuttled to a stand, drumstick dangling from his fingers. "Well, look at you, with your new, um, accoutrement—"

"Shut up!" Woggle's eyes narrowed. "You know what I want."

The other Messengers scooted from the doctor.

Dr. Hogger pointed to Woggle with the drumstick.

It sizzled near Woggle's finger.

"Yes," said the doctor, "but—good news! I just received approval to add a fifth Messenger."

"Did you?" said Fargar. "When?"

Dr. Hogger pointed the smoldering drumstick at Fargar. "Just before lunch. I was about to tell you." He turned to Woggle. "And now I'm telling you."

Woggle eased his shoulders. "What are you saying?"

Hogger smiled and raised the drumstick, as if conducting an orchestra. "Why not return to my office, where I can reevaluate you for team Messenger?"

Woggle sat on the exam table, but didn't bother to undress. "Why's it so dusty in here?"

Dr. Hogger didn't respond. He eyed him through his tinted goggles and pounded sections of a form with his personal stamp.

The doctor turned the parchment over. "They changed it. I must now rate your gimmick. You may think it's obvious, but I still must ask. What is it?"

"Gimmick? Axe-throwing."

Dr. Hogger paused. "Really?"

"It's always been."

He waved his stamp over Woggle's flaming arm. "Not something else, perhaps more recent?"

"No."

Dr. Hogger shrugged. "Very well. Demonstrate, please."

"Sure." Woggle hopped down and grabbed his axe sacks. "Just toss one into your cabinet or counter top?"

"The wall's fine."

Woggle opened a sack and removed an axe with his flaming arm. He readied a throw.

Smoke billowed from the handle.

"Um," said Hogger, "you might have a slight—"

"Oh, no!" Woggle dropped the axe.

The handle burned up, leaving an iron axe head.

"I—I just got to throw 'em quicker."

He grabbed another one, and flung it at the wall, but the angle was bad, and it bounced off.

The handle burned up, anyway.

And the sack burned up, spilling the rest of his axes on the floor.

Woggle smacked his hands to his face. "I can't do it."

"Woggle!" shouted Hogger. "You'll burn yourself!"

Woggle's flaming and non-flaming hands remained squished against his cheeks. "I can't burn myself with my own hand, now, can I?"

"Um, I'd disagree, but if you say so."

Woggle pounded the exam table with his normal hand. "What's the use? How can an axe-thrower throw an axe when they burn up every time he touches one?"

"Just to be clear, this axe-thrower is you, right?"

"Yes, it's me!" Woggle shook his head. "I'll never be a Messenger again. Just give me my bone back, and I'll leave."

Dr. Hogger lowered his clipboard.

"Maybe I could rejoin the army. Of course, they pack 'em together so tight, I'd burn the guy next to me."

The doctor's face blanked.

"I could ask for special permission to be placed on the far end of... what're you doing?"

In a haunting monotone, Dr. Hogger said, "The bone is mine."

Woggle sneered. "No, it's not. It's my bone. I found it."

"It is my payment for examining you—and saving your life."

"Yeah, well, a lot of good that did. I can't be on team Messenger, and—you're the reason I almost died! I demand a refund."

Dr. Hogger's jaw tightened. He leaned forward. "I claimed the bone by your own terms: I pried it from your dead, cold fingers."

Woggle balled up a fiery fist. "Do these fingers look cold and dead to you?"

The exam room door burst open. Fepig entered. "Make way."

"Um...," said Woggle.

The small orc pulled out three drawers at different lengths, creating a make-shift staircase. He climbed onto the counter top and removed a framed parchment.

Dr. Hogger spun to Fepig. "What are you doing?"

"Revoking your license." Fepig traipsed down the drawer-stairs.

Hogger threw his arms in the air. "Why?"

Fepig rose to his full (still short) height. "You haven't seen a patient in two months."

"I've been training! With Messenger!"

Fepig bore a sunny smile. "Good! You still have a job."

"But—but who else can be...?"

A rising squeak drew near.

A rickety wheelchair bumped the door wide open. "Ah, my first patient," said the chair's occupant. "You can call me Dr. Stubbins."

The new doctor jammed his leg stumps into a pair of bone stilts, and with grabbers on his arm stumps, he placed his medical license on the wall. He slid a grabber-prong across the counter's surface. "Why's it so dusty?"

"No one's been in here for months," said Fepig.

"Oh, well." Stubbins swapped a grabber with a feather duster attachment and cleared the counter.

"You can't do this!" said Hogger.

"What, dust?" said Dr. Stubbins.

Hogger whipped out a bonesaw in each hand. "No, replace me."

"I am replacing you."

"Gah!" Hogger stomped in place. "No, the thing you can't do is replace me." He raised a saw. "Now get out or—"

Woggle grabbed Hogger by the throat with his normal hand and reared back a fiery fist. "Or what?"

"Chop my limbs off?" Stubbins wiggled his feather duster. "Dragon beat ya to it."

Hogger dropped the saws. "Or—," he croaked. "Or—let go, let go. I won't do anything."

Woggle released him.

Hogger rubbed his throat. "Fine. I'll leave. But you'll never find that bone without—"

"Found it." Dr. Stubbins held open a cabinet door with a grabber, revealing the bone.

"So, I haven't had time to hide it properly." Hogger grinned. "But how can your new beloved doctor part with such a fine specimen?"

"This?" Stubbins snagged the bone with his grabber. "You can have it." He tossed it.

Woggle caught it—with his fiery hand.

"Oh, no!" he dropped it.

The bone clattered on the floor, luster still silvery.

Woggle blinked. "It didn't burn. It's not even scorched."

Hogger's jaw hung loose. "What kind of bone is it?"

"Dragon, you numskull," said Dr. Stubbins.

"How—how could you give it up so easily?"

"Yeah," said Woggle. "Don't you want it, too?"

Fepig dug the toe of his little boot in the floor. "I want it."

"Bah," said Stubbins. "Sure, they're rare, but when you've worked the Thousand-Thousand-Thousand[†] Bone Boneyard as long as I have, you can scrounge up a couple hundred of these."

Woggle's eyes widened. "Hundred?"

Hogger's eyes might have widened, too, under his goggles. "Couple?"

Woggle raised the bone with his fiery arm. "I—I could forge an axe head, and use this as the handle."

"Would you like a dozen more to fill your axe sacks?" said Stubbins.

"Would I?"

"Hey, don't repeat that around Umpi."

"Why not?"

"His false eye—made of wood."

"Come on, Hogger," said Fepig. "Time to go."

The former doctor slouched and followed Fepig out. They shut the door.

"Now," Dr. Stubbins waved a stamp in his grabber, "I'll need to fill out a new form with my mark. So, Woggle—"

"No." Woggle waggled his eyebrows. "Call me..."

~~FIREARM~~

DRAGON-AXE

[†] Not even Hete is familiar with terms like million or billion.

Fire Dance—An Invocation of the Light

Freddy Niagara Fonseca

I

Glow, fire, glow.
Whisper, crackle, shimmer.
Grow, fire, grow, grow.
Sparkle, illumine, glimmer.
Soar, fire, soar.
Reach higher, higher. Dance!
Illumine, illuminate, oh luminous fire.
Illuminate, oh Goddess, illumine us all.
We kindle the fire and once every year,
in the night of surrender,
we gather to worship the Goddess in secret
with magic, fire, and dance
by the radiant light on the face of the moon.

II

Singe, fire, singe.
Glisten, hiss and sizzle.
Leap, fire, leap, leap.
Radiate, scintillate, dazzle.
Dance, fire, dance.
Go higher, higher. Shine!
We've chosen the virgin. Her eyes are fire.
Enliven, oh virgin, enliven us all.
We're painted all over in screaming colors.
We glow like embers.
We glitter, gleaming at night,
and tremble in front of the Goddess of fire and doom
by the terrible light on the face of the moon.

III

Rage, fire, rage!
Soar and glisten. Roar.
Blaze, fire, blaze, blaze.
Fill us with luster. Soar.
Intenser, intenser. Burn.
Shine, fire, shine brighter!
Encircle, oh fire, encircle us all.
We glare and pant and growl. Nothing will stop us,
and from the bottom of the pit,
and out of the blackest of shadows, the devils arise
to revel in row after row with the ghosts of the dead,
and slowly a cloud of sulphur and dread
enshrouds the face of the moon.

IV

Glare, fire, glare.
Beat, drummers, beat, beat.
The witch doctor screams!
The sounds of hundreds of
pounding bare feet on the ground
and hammering fists and knuckles on drums
rebound and cut through the jungle around us,
engulfing, enthralling, ensnaring us all.
We watch an inferno and dance like demons—
the virgin screams!
We prance and growl, completely in trance;
we shake and crawl to the Goddess
and sprawl by the light of flaming surrender and fire.

V

Burn, fire, burn.
Roast and blister. Scorch.
The spirits of fire squirm
and dance on pyre and torch.
As the moon reappears,
we pray for redemption and

dash to the flames to fearlessly dance on the coals.
We cleanse ourselves—each soul is redeemed.
The sacrificed blood of the virgin is boiled.
The scent appeases the nostrils of Her,
the Goddess of fire, and reaches to all of the stars
in the vault of the sky by the blood red light
on the face of the moon.

VI

Glow, fire, glow.
And now we lie down
by the fire and dream.
Glow, fire, glow. Life is a dream,
a brittle illusion—when is it real?
Glow, fire, glow.
Before we know, life will be over.
Glow, surround us, oh, fire, envelop us all.
And light will brighten each feature.
Warmth will kindle each heart. The glow
of stars will show the heavenly eyes
of the Goddess of fire on high by the light
on the luminous face of the moon.

VII

Great Goddess of fire,
soaring higher, higher.
Who has beheld your
splendor and lived?
Oh Goddess, radiant, vibrant and bright—
we're awed by your grandeur—your
eyes are millions of stars—your face is the
sky all ablaze, igniting us all.
Your essence now fills our being—
we love and adore you.
At last we come to ourselves to laugh,
to sing and to reel. The sky is a witness to joy

by the glorious light on the face of the moon.

VIII

    Sing, fire, sing.
    The light of the stars
    has touched every soul.
    The children come forward with
    garlands, palm leaves, and fruits.
    Sing, fire. Sing, dance.
Illumine, illuminate, oh magical fire.
Illuminate, oh Spirit, illumine us now.
We chant with angels, seraphs, and gods.
We're sinless and free.
We rise to the One, the highest of all.
We dwell in ourselves, and we know, and we bow
to the glimmering light in the east—to the dawn . . .

IX

    Glow, fire, glow.
    And here comes the dawn,
    the mystical dawn.
    Rise, fire, rise over death.
    And here comes the sun, the glorious sun.
    Today is the day of peace and surrender.
We rise from the shadows—we rise from the night.
We look to the East—we reach for the Light.
Oh Light, oh all-seeing Light,
eternal, boundless, loving and bright.
Illumine, illuminate, oh all-knowing Light.
Illumine, illuminate, ignite now, oh Light.
Ignite the spark that has lived and endured in us all.

52

Divine Light
Laura Goldman Weinberg

Holy Fire
Laura Goldman Weinberg

The fire that does not consume
What is it?

I see You in it
It surrounds You
Encompasses You

Yet You remain the same
What is it?

Moses saw it in the bush
The burning bush that did not burn

And I see You
Sitting in lotus

In the fire of fires
The holy of holies
Is You

You consume me

Burn everything
Till there is only You

Let me be consumed in the fire
Of Your love
Till even the ashes dissolve
Into infinity
And we are one
Forever
In the ocean of consciousness

Burn me
Till I am gone

And only You exist
For all time

The Eternal Flame
Daniel Brawner

"I burn! I burn!" Bob muttered to himself. "With each passing day, the slow, cruel combustion of cell metabolism gnaws away at my extremities. The pale skiff of my ashes trails behind me, proof that I am doomed, little more than a dead thing."

"Can I put my arm down now, Bobby? This is starting to hurt."

Bob glanced up from the camera's viewfinder and blinked hard. "Sorry, Mom. Sure. I think I got the shot."

"I know it's only a Styrofoam torch. It's not really heavy, but geez! I never thought I would feel pity for the Statue of Liberty," she said. She shook her arm limply and removed the spiky, tin foil tiara with her other hand. A small Franklin stove with a glass door flickered in the corner of the room. It was chilly for early November.

"Okay, we're done for today. But you know how important it is for me to preserve you on film. Because…someday…." The words got caught in his throat.

"Was she always green? I mean, she didn't start out that way, did she? Ms. Liberty? Look! My torch arm is turning green, don't you think?"

Bob rolled his eyes and gently slipped the medium-format Hasselblad back into its case. "You're not taking this seriously."

"You gotta lighten up, Bobby. You can't go on like this. One minute, you're chatting with the customers like a normal person and the next minute you're ranting like a wild-eyed prophet about entropy— whatever that is. Clients are starting to complain." A light drizzle tapped on the skylight. She reached for her umbrella and winced with a quick intake of breath.

"Are you all right, Mom?"

She grinned. "Right as rain, Bobby. Right as rain."

***

"Now let's see that thousand-yard stare," Bob said encouragingly.

The client Gerald was doing his best to look like the future father of the country in Emanuel Leutze's painting of Washington Crossing the Delaware, with one foot up on a disguised orange crate in the cardboard boat, one hand clutching at a rumpled gray robe. It had taken him a half hour to get into the 18th Century costume with all the buttons. Gerald was posing for a résumé he hoped would land him a good job as a personnel director. He squinted into the back wall of Bob's "Ye Olde Photo Shoppe," located near historic Colonial Williamsburg. Bob specialized in Early American-themed portraits. Gerald glanced over at Bob. "How's this?"

Bob sighed. "The robe thing isn't working. Try shading your eyes with that hand. You're a man of vision! Resolute! You see into the future. Easily worth sixty thousand a year! And grit your teeth."

Gerald brightened and complied. "Ow! Sorry, I bit my lip." He gamely continued to gaze resolutely across the frozen Delaware. "Should I smile?"

Bob looked up from the camera monitor. "Smile? What for? Washington wasn't smiling in that boat, was he? And do you know why?"

Gerald shrugged. "He was cold?"

"He was going to die!"

Gerald flinched but continued to stare. "He didn't die though, did he?"

Bob exhaled impatiently. "Well, not then. Later, he did."

"I mean, they won and everything. And America became a country. So, at least Washington did something important before he died."

"What difference does that make?" Bob demanded. "That's just stuff that happens—like the wind blowing from the west or your shoe coming untied. The point is that no matter what we do, we die."

Gerald dropped the hand shading his eyes from the hot studio lights and the imaginary campfires of the murderous, though unsuspecting, Hessian army bivouacked on the other side of the river. "Yeah, I guess so."

"There's no guessing to it," said Bob, revving up. "Death is the only certainty. You're dying right now."

"I feel fine," Gerald said, though suddenly, he was not so sure.

"Death and life are interconnected, inseparable. Like fire and heat. From the moment we're born, the flame of Death is lit within us, warming our blood in the gentle hearth that will one day grow to become a raging funeral pyre!"

Gerald shivered and glanced longingly at the Franklin stove.

"The harder we strive and the more we achieve, the hotter we burn so that even the furnace of our body is consumed in the blaze."

"My doctor warned me to cut down on the calories," Gerald said, his plumpness straining at the double row of buttons on his George Washington waistcoat.

"Sure, we try to tend the fire," Bob continued, flushed, "control it, make it last. But, in the end, the fuel runs out and the flame is extinguished. Have you ever heard of the term 'entropy', Gerald?"

"That's one of those thermodynamic laws, isn't it?" Gerald remembered about as much from high school chemistry as he did the baffling labyrinth of inflected endings from German class.

"That's right. It's the Second Law of Thermodynamics. It means —I don't really understand it—but it means that heat will move toward anything cold and that everything is slowly and inevitably falling apart."

"Including us?"

"Including us. Exactly! It's like the fragile architecture of Order cannot withstand the strain of Chaos and eventually something's got to give."

At that moment, a button from the George Washington vest popped off, pinged across the studio and slid to rest against the orange and yellow painted simulated flame of the Statue of Liberty torch. "I could have seen that coming," Gerald wheezed, struggling to draw a deep breath under the constraints of the costume.

"I have a dark confession," said Bob, ignoring the rebellious button.

Gerald looked apprehensive, holding up two pudgy hands in protest. "Hey, now Mr. Lacey, you don't need to admit anything to me. About death or whatever. Some secrets should remain secret—am I right? I mean, whatever you're guilty of...."

"I have an incurable disease."

Gerald stiffened. "What?"

"There's nothing that can be done."

"What is it?" asked Gerald, suddenly concerned.

"I don't like to talk about it," said Bob, staring across the Delaware. "Gerald, have you ever thought about how a person starts out young, healthy and strong? Then after a certain age, things begin falling apart? Skin wrinkles, muscles sag, men's hair falls out?"

Gerald involuntarily reached for the shiny spot on his head but the blue Napoleon-style hat blocked his hand.

"After the age of about 30, we stop thriving and start to wither. What do they call it—'the arrow of time'? It goes up at first. Then down, down, down. And there's nothing we can do!" Bob snapped his fingers.

"Hey, you want to try a photo from a different angle? How about I shoot from down low and make you look huge?"

Gerald plucked off the hat and dropped it behind the cardboard boat. "You know what? I've decided I don't want that job after all. Maybe I'll take a year off. Travel. Join a monastery. Take up drinking. Best of luck to you. And everything," he added significantly. He fiddled in vain with the buttons on the stiff jacket. "Why don't I just mail you this costume?"

***

Bob's mother sat in a rickety rocking chair in the middle of the studio, pretending to put the finishing touches on the original American flag with its thirteen stars arranged in a circle against a blue background. As Betsy Ross, she wore a simple white shawl over a brown cotton dress and a modest lace cap, befitting a proper Quaker lady. She pushed the oversized needle through the fabric of the flag.

"God damn it!" she yelped and sucked the injured index finger. "Sorry, Bobby. I just hate needles."

Bob looked up from his camera, amused. "Mom, you know you don't have to actually make the flag." He frowned. "You've never sewn anything in your life. Why would you hate needles?"

She stopped rocking. "And what's the deal with rocking chairs? How can anybody relax in a chair that won't stand still?" She rose unsteadily to her feet. "They're dangerous."

"Are you sure you're okay?" Bob stood up and took her arm, guiding her to a gilded wooden throne he had once used in a photo shoot of King George III, now in need of dusting and new paint. "Can I get you some water?"

His mother waved away the suggestion. "Don't fuss, Bobby."

Bob released her arm. "It's just that I worry about you, Mom. I wouldn't want you to fall and break a hip or something. You might not recover."

"And would you stop being so morbid? It's giving me the creeps."

Bob stared at the floor, looking morose. "I don't mean to be morbid, Mom. But you know I can hardly ignore that we are mortal. And fragile." He lowered his voice. "And I have an incurable disease."

His mother laid her hand on his shoulder. "Bobby, you've got psoriasis."

"And there's no cure!" he bleated in defense. He laid his hand on hers. Why had he not noticed the dark circles under her eyes? Up close, he could see that her face was pale, the skin tight over her cheekbones.

58

"Your hand is so cold." His mother tried to smile. "What is this bruise on your wrist?"

She shrugged. "It's where they draw the blood."

"You hate needles," Bob barely whispered.

"It's not so bad, really."

Bob felt a chill run through his body. "Tell me," was all he could manage. The stove was down to embers now.

"It's Stage Four. Pancreatic," she said matter-of-factly.

Bob felt like he was about to pass out. "Mom, are you telling me you're dying?"

She took him by the shoulders and looked into his eyes with a fierceness he had never seen in her before. "No, Bobby. I'm telling you I'm alive! I'm alive now. And so are you."

Bob looked helpless. "So, what do we do?"

She fluffed the homespun skirt derisively. "Well, the first thing I'm going to do is change out of this ugly dress and put on something nice. Then, you can take my picture—you know—not as Betsy Ross. But as I really am." She nodded toward the stove. "And for heaven's sake, Bobby. Throw some wood on the fire. It's freezing in here!"

Burning in the Heartland
Kristine Perkins

Helen limped down Main Street clutching a tin lunch pail. The walk from her dad's house to Mabel's Penny Store was four blocks, and the pregnancy made her ankles swell. Iowa's hot August weather, heavy with humidity, made matters worse. Folded white socks hid fat ankles but the leather saddle shoes were unforgiving and left deep, red grooves that itched at night. Pretty soon, Helen told her dad, she would need to work in his slippers.

"Over my dead body," he'd said, smoking a pipe in the dining room. He shut the Home Workshop Manual he was reading and let it clatter onto the walnut table. The table was a wedding gift 25 years earlier for his bride only because his neighbor needed someone to take the tree and dispose of it. He had only just started at B & A Lumber back then, but they lent him the equipment to fell the tree and haul it to his small workshop. The three weeks leading up to their nuptials, he spent bent over large slabs of dark wood, smoothing edges and planing wooden curlicues—as delicate looking as if they were made from chocolate shavings. Like they'd melt at the slightest touch of a warm finger.

He pointed his pipe toward the door. "You got yourself into this mess. You get yourself out."

Main Street was empty except for store owners sweeping the sidewalks, getting ready to unlock their doors. Helen paused in the shade of the overhang to catch her breath before opening the heavy wooden door that jangled the bell. Mabel's Penny Store had the largest store front in Rolling Rock, population 650. Helen considered herself lucky to have a job right after high school, and her father depended on her paycheck even more after Helen's mother died suddenly from a brain aneurysm a little over a year ago. Shortly after her mother passed away, Helen found out she was pregnant and married Wayne in late November during a rushed ceremony with cake and punch in the church basement. She quit her job the very next day.

The newly-married couple moved in with Wayne's family until they could find a place of their own, but a few weeks later, Pearl Harbor was bombed. Wayne enlisted, citing it his duty, and was now overseas somewhere, machining metal. He would miss the birth of his child. It took some convincing, but Mabel did hire Helen back, and Helen moved back in with her father and brother.

"Morning," Helen called. She slid her lunch pail behind the counter and sat on the stool Mabel had brought up for her to rest while she managed the register.

"Morning." Mabel emerged from the back and handed her a stack of handkerchiefs to set out in the window display. "Traffic heavy?" she asked.

Helen heaved herself up and limped over to the window. "Awful," she said, playing into the joke. She saw three cars, and Rolling Rock only had four stop signs in the whole town. *At least they didn't have horses and buggies anymore,* Helen thought, or she'd have to watch out for horse manure each morning. She had ruined a pair of shoelaces once after the Fourth of July parade because the street cleaner let the horse droppings sit for a day. The manure wouldn't wash out no matter how much elbow grease, castile soap, and Ajax she used.

"New treatment?" Helen asked, referring to Mabel's hair.

Ever since they were little girls, Mabel always had the most recent hair styles and visited Miss Cora's Salon whenever she fancied because it was right next to her father's store. Mabel's father would do anything for his only daughter—even change the name of his family store upon her birth from G.H. Pullman's General Store to Mabel's Penny Store. He argued it was strictly a business decision to drum up new customers and draw in out-of-towners, but everyone knew it was because of her.

"Oh, yes." Mabel touched her hair and looked out the window. Mr. Jacobs held the door open for Mrs. Harold Hansen to walk into the bank. Little Johnnie Johnson raced by on his bike, cutoff jean shorts, no shirt, and a raccoon tail hat. The summer sun had already risen to 'It's too hot out for that.'

"Now how can that boy wear a hat like that on a day like today?" Mabel asked.

Helen watched the boy slow down at the intersection, look both ways, and pedal on his merry way toward the creek and the old railroad track. All the kids went down to catch crawdads despite Sheriff Pals' continuous warnings about how dangerous it was.

"Then take it out," the townspeople had said. "It's county-owned."

"We've got more important things to focus on at the moment," said Pals, knowing there were no funds or staff to dismantle it.

Helen smoothed out the last handkerchief and rested her hands on the back of the display case. She left Mabel's comment hanging in the air, like a loosened spider web untethered on one end.

Mabel changed the subject. "There's something I've been meaning to talk to you about."

Helen crossed her arms and looked out the large glass window, past Mabel, to see her brother, Otto, come around the corner and head for the door. It was morning, and he would be sober but in a hungover, nasty mood. Helen held up a hand to pause Mabel's next words and pointed to the door.

Otto pushed open the door, barely missing Mabel who scooted out of the way at the last second. He glared at the counter and then scanned the store, hardly taking in the greeting cards, two different men's leather shoes—one black, one brown—and the tins of shoe polish to go along with them. Otto's eyes settled on his very pregnant sister. He let the door close, jangling the bell.

"Hi," Helen said, trying to lighten the mood. She glanced at Mabel whose jaw tightened.

"Where'd you put 'em?" he asked, not bothering to look at his sister's boss. During their school days, Otto was sweet on Mabel: the most beautiful girl in town. It took him a whole year to work up the courage to ask her to the Homecoming dance, and it took her thirty seconds to laugh in his face in the cafeteria. Others pointed and laughed along with her. At that moment, he stopped liking her for looks. He started hating the person she was.

"Put what?" Helen swished her hands on either side of her dress, feeling the light cotton fabric she picked out to make maternity clothes— a beautiful yellow. Wayne's favorite color.

"The keys," Otto said.

"Should be in the ignition." Helen shrugged and stuck out her bottom lip.

"They're not," her brother said. A mist of spit made a rainbow that hung briefly in the morning light, sprinkling the wooden floorboards, some landing on his dusty work boots. "God damn it. You know God damn well where they are. You're costing me my job." Otto took two steps forward and poked his index finger at her belly.

Helen stepped back. Her heel caught on a ripple in the floorboard seam, which sent her falling into the shelf of canned saltine crackers. Her hands reached out for her brother. He did not move.

"Oh, my God." Mabel bent down and said to Otto, "Help me."

Otto hooked a hand under Helen's armpit. Mabel did the same on the other side. Together, they lifted Helen and guided her over to the stool by the counter.

"I didn't take your keys," Helen said, clutching her belly. "Maybe they're under the seat."

Otto stormed out the door and shoved his hands deep in his jean pockets, heading toward Tally's Grill.

"Can I get you water?" Mabel wrung her hands and fiddled with her necklace, an opal she had received for their high school graduation from her parents. It was the same opal Helen had eyed each time she worked after school stocking shelves. The late-afternoon sun always glinted off the gold chain from across the hazy store, sometimes blinding Helen as she counted back change for hair nets and Spam. During breaks, she dusted the jewelry case just to get a glimpse of the creamy white gem with light pink swirls. According to the latest *Woman's Day*, light pink complemented fair skin with warm undertones, which described Helen best. There weren't enough hours in the work week for Helen to earn it herself, and there was no way her parents could afford such a luxury—even for a celebration such as graduation.

Instead, Helen got a sweet card with purple flowers and a leather-bound journal from her mother. Both of which stayed tucked under Helen's mattress. The last entry was dated June 27, 1941.

Mother died.

The page was smudged from Helen's tears as they dripped. She hadn't the strength to wipe them away.

"Here." Mabel handed Helen a coffee mug. "Water. Not coffee."

"Thanks." Helen took a sip even though she wasn't thirsty. She knew Mabel liked to feel useful.

A customer walked in, took one look at the cans littering the floor, and said, "What happened?"

Mabel giggled nervously. "Don't mind the mess. Just a small slip. Please." She came out from behind the counter and let her hand, palm up, showcase the rest of the store. "Feel free to look around. We'll get that cleaned up soon. Just watch your step."

The customer, a person neither of them had ever seen before, gave them a small smile and turned to leave. "I'll come back."

Mabel pinched her lips together and crossed her arms. She turned back toward the counter. "You're sure you're alright?"

Helen nodded. "Just need to rest."

Mabel looked up at the ceiling. "Maybe this is the perfect segue then. There's never a good time to do this, so why not now? Of all days?

"Listen, you're a smart girl, and you should know this has been coming for some time. Sales have slowed." She motioned toward the door and guffawed. "And with your condition, I think it's best if you focus on your family for now."

"You're letting me go?" Helen asked.

"Unfortunately, yes. And I want you to know that I would keep you on if we needed you, but daddy's been doing the books, and business-wise, it just doesn't make sense. Gotta trim the fat." Mabel smoothed her skirt and examined her nails for a long, pregnant pause.

"Could you at least wait until the baby comes?"

"That could be any moment, and we can't have any more damage done to our merchandise. It's not just the damage to the store." Mabel made eye contact and shrugged matter-of-factly. "You could get seriously hurt. There's no place here for a soon-to-be-mother. You're better off at home for both of your sakes."

Helen wobbled down the road back to her empty house. Once she got inside and unpacked the lunch pail, put away the food, and tucked the container under the sink, letting the homemade cloth curtain she'd sewn out of a torn bed sheet fall back into perfectly-pleated place, she sat down at the dining room table.

Ever since her mother died, Helen did her best to keep the house picked up for her dad and brother. The other three sisters were married and lived on farms in the surrounding area and helped when they could, but Rose, Muriel, and Eileen had their hands full with their own babies and laundry and meals to cook and curtains to wash and beds to make and faces to wipe and husbands to serve. One of the battles Helen stopped fighting was keeping the mail stacked on one side of the walnut table. Along with the yellow and white envelopes, there were fresh pieces of stationary and a fountain pen. She licked a finger and laid it on the top sheet which pulled away from the stack without effort. Next, she took up the pen and went to writing, head bent and foot shaking up and down.

Dear Wayne, she wrote. *I miss you more today than yesterday. And I hope this finds you well and in good spirits. Baby is fine and dropped even more. How is that possible? Ready any day now. I was fired from Mabel's this morning, but you shouldn't worry. We've got enough food to eat and the house is paid for. Rain yesterday but bright and sunny skies today. They say we're supposed to get rain the next seven days, and we need it. You said you thought you'd see a lot of rain. Is that true? Are you getting enough to eat? With all my love, Helen*

Helen creased the letter with one quick swipe of her thumb and licked the envelope, hoping the news wouldn't worry Wayne. She only told him because she never wanted to keep secrets from the man she married. With a deep breath to steady her shaking hand, Helen addressed it in her best penmanship. Wayne always replied, but the last letter went without a response. This time she was going to make sure they could read her handwriting and get this letter to her husband. She knew he was safe since she hadn't gotten a death notification telegram.

With no plans for the rest of the day, she went about making a list of the baby things she still needed and made sure the bassinet's sheets were still spotless—no dust in sight. It was set up right next to her bed. On the dresser, a soft hairbrush, a rattle with a silky green ribbon tied just so, and a stack of cloth diapers were lined in a neat row. All borrowed from Rose who had twin girls who were 20 months.

"If I hear that rattle one more time, I may go insane," Rose guffawed over church coffee earlier that spring, urging Helen to take them from her home.

Helen picked up the rattle and shook it. *Must be dried rice inside,* she thought.

Heaving herself onto her bed, she promptly fell asleep, letting her fingers touch the wooden rails of the bassinet, imagining a little girl or boy sleeping next to her, keeping her company.

It wasn't until her father came home early from the lumberyard that she woke up. It was half past one o'clock in the afternoon. Her stomach rumbled.

"What're you doing here?" her father asked. He stood by the back door and lit his pipe.

"You're not going to believe this. I got fired this morning." She dug out her peanut butter sandwich that was wrapped in parchment paper from earlier and took a bite.

Her father's voice stayed steady. "What in the hell'd that happen for?" He puffed and waved the lit match back and forth to extinguish the flame, smoke tendrils creating dragon's tails and the smoke clouds of her youth. Helen stayed put and let the cherry flavored-tobacco wash over her large belly and breathed deep. She loved the smell and could finally tolerate it again late in pregnancy. During the first trimester, she practically locked herself in her room to get away from it wafting throughout the whole house.

Helen shrugged and poured herself some whole milk, holding the glass milk bottle out to her dad who shook his head. She replaced the cap and put it back in the olive green Frigidaire.

"She never liked me anyway."

"Why's that?"

"Who knows. Could be anything."

"Now what're ya gonna do?" He put his hand on the doorknob.

"I don't know."

Later that evening, Otto came home singing Navy songs that washed Helen in whiskey breath at the stove.

"Dance with me," he said, taking up her hand and wrapping an arm around her waist. Helen almost lost her balance and pushed him away.

"Don't knock me over," she said.

He fell asleep over his dinner plate, and she helped her dad carry him to the couch. There was no way anyone would get that big guy upstairs to his bed.

After the dishes sat in the drying rack and the table wiped clean of crumbs, Helen finally sat in the living room. She sketched out her to-do list:

- Eggs/feed chickens
- Mail letter to Wayne
- Mend pile of pants
- Scrub floors
- Sweep upstairs
- Dust the China cabinet
- Make bread
- Start kringla dough
- Visit Mabel - change mind?

As a pregnant lady does, Helen collapsed in her bed but woke two hours later to pee. Or—what was that? It sounded like it came from the kitchen. Probably just Otto, she told herself. She descended the stairs, quietly, avoiding the creaky spots. The front door was open, and splayed out on the rug was the hall tree, knocked over and leaning against the opposite wall, a hole in the plaster her father would be none too pleased to fix.

She quickly checked the couch. Otto was gone. She lifted the hall tree back up. Her dad came down the stairs.

"What happened?" he asked, securing an overall strap with a click.

"Otto's gone." She closed the door. "I gotta go to the bathroom."

The night was stifling, and the air was still. With all the windows open in the house, Helen could smell the Lily of the Valley just outside the bathroom, by the back door steps. Their white bells looked best in the early morning dew that made them sparkle in the sunlight, like the small diamond she wore that Wayne scraped together for their shotgun wedding right before he left for the war. The same war that she prayed each night wouldn't take him away.

The baby kicked. Helen paused and wondered when she'd get to meet the little one.

"Hey, little guy," she cooed. There was no doubt in her mind it was a boy. Without proof, it was easy to get her hopes up. And she hated to agree with Mabel, but it could be any day now. What was she thinking continuing to work this close to her due date? Helen wiped and stood, pulling her underwear up under her pillowy nightgown. Her large breasts were almost visible through the white linen. Funny she didn't think anything of it when her dad came down the stairs. Just as she reached around to flush, faintly, through the window, she heard glass shattering.

She flicked the light switch off and peered out into the dark corn field, half expecting to see Otto passed out in the grass. Maybe chicken feed would be pressed against his face or a puddle of vomit would reflect the bright moonlight.

"Did you hear that?" Helen didn't bother washing her hands but crossed her arms across the thin nightgown and sat on the couch. Her dad sat in the rocking chair. In the dark.

"Yeah." He stuck a pinkie finger in his ear and wiggled, yawning and stretching his jaw to reach deeper into the ear canal. Finally, after it seemed he found what he was after, he wiped the pinkie on the thigh of his overalls.

A bad taste developed in Helen's throat. The thought of earwax made her stomach feel like a washing machine stuck on agitate. She swallowed and looked out the window.

"'Spose it's Otto?" she asked.

"Could be."

"Think he's hurt?"

"Naw," he said. "He's fine. Go back to bed."

"Think he's outside?"

"I'll check it out."

Helen did as she was told and got to bed but could not find a comfortable position. She peeled her sweaty thighs apart and stuffed the extra pillow between her knees. The air was so stale in her room, she thought she might stop breathing when she did finally fall asleep. The curtains were still. Crickets deafening in their crescendo. Through the window screen, her dad's feet swished through the grass. She heard him lift the old canoe by the shed. He slammed the shed door. It bounced a few times before resting in a half-open fashion, Helen imagined. Chickens clucked, roused from their slumber.

Heartburn crept up Helen's throat. She swallowed spice. Swallowed twice. A third time, wishing it away. Her dad came back inside. She sat up and stuffed more blankets behind her pillow and leaned it against the headboard so she could prop herself up. But it was no use. She needed water.

As she sat all the way up, she looked out the south-facing window. The same window she could see across the street and into their neighbor's house. It was also the direction she walked to work. There was no need to notice the bright night sky or the moon glinting off the neighbor's wind chime. It was too big to ignore and too unusual to place. A small glow coming from Main Street. A glow too orange to be headlights. Too large to be a flashlight or a streetlamp or anything other than a fire.

A fire truck whirred, growing louder as it got closer to the fire.

Helen tumbled out of bed and pulled on her silky robe, conscious of anyone glimpsing her dark nipples through her nightgown. She slid into a spare pair of her brother's work boots and clobbered down the front steps, holding the railing with shaking hands, her father on her heels.

He raced ahead as she fast-walked as hard as she could, stopping twice to ease the baby's foot out of her ribcage. Porch lights and neighbors flooded the streets, asking each other questions that no one could answer.

"Is there a fire?"

"Is it a drill?"

"'Spose it's the bank?"

The most news-worthy thing to happen in all of Rolling Rock, ever, was a freak airplane landing in Fred Cummings' corn field in the summer of '34. The pilot had gotten such a bad migraine, he couldn't tell where his landing strip was, so he gave a Hail Mary and got out of the sky as fast as he could, landing the plane without bursting into flames, but taking out acres of corn. It was still the talk of the town.

With just one block to go, Helen heard the yells. She knew that shout. When she rounded the corner, there were more than firefighters putting out the fire at Mabel's. Police officers were cuffing Otto and shoving him into their cruiser. Her dad stood on the sidewalk, across the street from Mabel's and lit a cigarette. He waved good-bye to his son who silently yelled from the back of the police car behind closed windows. He was going to the county jail.

"What happened?" she asked her dad.

He turned and pointed a finger at her. "What'd you do?"

Firemen came over to the small crowd that had gathered and waved their arms, pushing them back from the heat of the flames.

Helen looked at the large orange monster. Heat from the building licked her legs and burned her cheeks, already rosy from the walk. Her nose tingled and tears formed. She blinked them back when she saw Mabel get out of a car and scream as she fell to her knees. Mabel's dad ran over and tried to take over the water hose, as if the firefighter was missing all the spots that should be put out. Like watching a toddler color and knowing you'd do it differently. You'd fill in the tips of the birds' wings before the chest and the tail before the head.

"This is your fault," Helen's father said and flicked his cigarette.

Braille bumps of sweat decorated her father's forehead, and his tanned face looked black against the midnight glow.

"What?" Helen grabbed a lapel of the robe and gathered the neck closed.

A calloused finger hovered before the tip of her nose.

"Don't lie," he hissed. "You said something to him."

"I didn't say anything," Helen said, "nothing."

People closest to them looked their way, backing away from her father who had gotten right up next to Helen, puffing up his chest and looming over her.

"First *that*." He aimed his finger at the baby. "And now *this*." He pointed at the flames that had reached the top of the building—which was almost halfway up the water tower just two blocks away.

"You'd better call a sister tomorrow because you're out of my house. For good," he said.

Orange flames whipped back and forth in her father's eyes. He walked away. Helen could not move. She could not speak. She could not cry. All she heard was the crackling of the wooden beams collapsing as the ceiling fell in chunks. Mabel's father yelled. The crowd gasped. And now that the roof was gone, new pockets of air fueled the fire into unpredictable waves that reached for the sky and the stars—themselves fireballs.

Helen looked at the moon and wondered if Wayne was seeing the same sky. Was he asleep or awake? Alone or with a friend. Thinking of her. Of the baby. Making plans for his return. Helen wondered if they'd have more babies. She hoped so. And if they had a bastard grandson, it would never know it. They would be loved and welcomed and get just as many Christmas gifts as all the other grandbabies.

Helen felt a quick, dull pop deep in her belly. Water trickled down her leg and into Otto's boot.

"He's coming," she said to the woman next to her.

Screaming from Inside the Flames

Jill Cronbaugh

I stand amidst the kindling
Screaming from inside the flames

I am who I am!
I love whom I love!

Rainbow bodies slowly advance
Encircling the fiery core of fear

You live in the putrefying past!
You will die consumed by vitriol!

Scorn scorches me
Hatred sets my purple hair ablaze

How is this hurting YOU?!
Why do you care where I pee?!

I cradle the young one
Tender skin pocked with blisters

Look at what you have done!
How can you hurt something so precious?!

I offer the cherished to the Rainbow
Watching the burn marks become armor under the colorful balm

THERE is the FUTURE!
THERE is acceptance and love!

Standing on glowing embers
I peer through the spiking flares

There are more of us than you can imagine!
You cauterize yourself for no reason!

Rainbow hands touch fever-mad hearts
Sweet relief blooms as flames recede

We are who we are.
Love us as we are.

Oh, to Burn!
Megan Walsh

It started with a candle.

Chelsea felt the lighter's metal ribs under her thumb, the fast-click-then-flame. She watched the wick bloom as the flame caught. The heat licked at her skin.

***

Every Wednesday she went to the historic brick building on Downriver Avenue and saw Chaz, her counselor, (she refused to call him her "therapist" or "psychologist," and if she ever brought him up in conversation she referred to him as her "friend," which was a better lie). On her first visit, he asked why she decided to start therapy.

Chelsea ran her fingers along the edge of the cushions where the fabric had pilled under other patients' fingers. "How old is this building?"

"1980s maybe," Chaz said.

The popcorn ceiling reminded her of the one-bedroom Cleveland apartment she shared with her mom as a child. The apartment was subsidized by the government and a temporary escape the first time they left her mother's boyfriend.

Chelsea still hadn't talked to Chaz about her mother's boyfriend.

Chaz scratched his chin. "How about this, what might you like to talk about in our sessions?"

Chelsea closed her eyes and thought about the candle her mother's boyfriend bought her at Winterfest. It smelled like pine and the wax was green like the house across the street—a not-quite-right-green, too bright, too fake, too in-your-face. It was one of the last in a line of gifts: a Betty-Spaghetti, Doodle Bear, Polly Pocket, panties. Chelsea always said, "Thank you," as she looked at the ground and her mother smiled behind her boyfriend, nodded, *Yes, yes, it's very nice, thank you so much.*

Chelsea looked at Chaz. "I'm only here because I have to be. Court-ordered or whatever."

Chaz set down his pen and crossed his legs. "Would you rather we sat in silence for the next hour?"

The room was off-white with plants hanging from macrame

holders in the windows. Children's books and toys were stacked in the corner opposite the couch and Chelsea could see *Letter City and the Alphabet Winds* set next to a Spanish translation of *Goodnight, Moon.* Two men yelled at each other on the street below.

"What do you want to know?" she asked.

"We can start from the beginning," Chaz said. "Tell me about your mom."

***

Raylynn was a small woman, no taller than five foot two, with a laugh bigger than her stature. She wore gold hoop earrings, stage makeup, and teased her hair inches up from the crown of her head. When she wasn't swearing at morning talk show hosts or spilling booze on the futon, Raylynn was at the bar throwing her head back and thrusting her chest in the air.

As far as her mother's boyfriends went, Derek wasn't so bad. He bought Chelsea's mother jewelry and took them downtown to the Merry-Go-Round on school nights. His smile wasn't entirely crooked and his hair was clean and pressed into a proper part. Chelsea's mother laughed big and loud when Derek whispered in her ear. When she did this, Chelsea wanted to gather everyone around to see. "Look!" she'd say, "Look how happy we are!"

***

"Will you tell me about the first item you set on fire?" Chaz asked.

It had only been a piece of paper, ripped from a school notebook. Those blank-lined pages were inconsequential; she just wanted to know what would happen, how quickly the flame would travel from one corner to the other. That time, she filled the plastic bucket her mom used for soaking her feet to put out the fire. What had been more satisfying? Watching the paper burn? Or the soda-fizz pssst of the spark on the water?

Chelsea told Chaz about the notebook paper.

"And how did it feel to watch it burn?" He asked.

She felt bored by his question and moved from laying on the couch to facing him. "Satisfying," she said.

After she burned the notebook paper, she burned the letters from her ex-boyfriend, then the roll of toilet paper, then the receipts her mom kept in a drawer by the fridge, then the panties her mother's boyfriend gave her. She paused before the panties and cleared the ashes from previous burns into a plastic garbage bin. She held the panties long enough for the flame to reach the purlicue of her right hand then dropped them, panicked, into the ashes of the waste bin. But she had wanted to keep them, in some way. So she scooped up the ashes and placed them in a plastic bag. The next day she went to a thrift store and picked out a wooden box with a dahlia engraved on the lid.

On the coffee table between her and Chaz, the box of ashes sat unopened. Chelsea lifted the lid and dug her fingers into the gray-black specks. "Wielding that amount of power is singular," she said.

***

After her sessions with Chaz, Chelsea went home and brewed a cup of lavender tea in the copper kettle she'd bought her ex-wife, Lauren. Her apartment was clean and minimal. The art on the wall consisted of sharp lines, and the only contours she kept were the rounded edges of furniture. Even those she preferred to be slight as the cusp of a crescent moon.

Lauren never knew that Chelsea burned receipts in the bathroom, and grew irritated when she locked the door.

"How are we supposed to be intimate when you lock me out?"

"We're intimate in other ways."

Chelsea always grabbed Lauren's hand to appease her, even though Lauren's hands were limp and clammy.

"I want to feel close to you," she said

"You're the closest person to me," Chelsea said.

If there was distance, it was in the space between Chelsea's fingertips, those small gaps that widened when she ran her palm down Lauren's back. It was the space between Lauren's lips, her thighs, where her wrists didn't quite meet her shoulders, raised over her head in bed, waiting, *come get me.*

She had been taught physical intimacy. Knew how to close the space between skin. But when Lauren lay next to her, sticky and out of breath, wanting to open up in other ways, Chelsea pulled back.

When the kettle whistled on the stove after her sessions, and Chelsea poured the water into her mug, she put the box of ashes on the coffee table and placed a candle on top like a centerpiece. Wisps of steam rose to her nose and the lavender soothed her. Most nights the yellow lighter lay on the edge of the coffee table and she'd grip the mug while rapping her fingers on the handle. She wouldn't do it. She was making progress. But maybe she could put her thumb on the wheel, press the small red button. How long had it been since she'd listened to the whizz of gas release from the small container?

***

On an overcast Monday, she tucked the lighter into her slacks to feel the hard outline against her thigh as she discussed ROI and analytics at work. She fingered the side of it as she sat in meetings. And once everyone left, she removed it from her pocket and set it in the middle of her desk.

The city glowed beyond the windows of her office. Lights flickered on and off across the avenue. People shouted on the street. Sirens wailed from the hospital.

When she looked at the lighter, she thought of her mother's boyfriend. It was November. Her mother had been working doubles and the boyfriend was her stand-in babysitter. He brought the candle, but when he realized she didn't have a lighter, he went to buy one.

"Yellow," he said, "happy, like you."

And then he flicked the metal-rib of the lighter and held it close to her face.

"Don't be afraid," he said, "I won't hurt you."

Then he lit the candle and turned off the lights.

Chelsea was enamored by the way the flame carried across the living room and cast shadows with the TV trays. She watched the darkness dance across the stained walls as if it were alive.

***

Chaz tapped his pen on the notepad. "And how did it feel when you saw your coworker on the other side of the glass?"

Chelsea stared at the small framed picture of a tabby cat on the side table. "I don't remember," she said.

He leaned toward her. "Please, Chelsea."

"He looked like a premonition."

When he sat back in the chair, it didn't make a sound.

"And then?"

It was all so loud. The alarms. The sprinklers. The screaming, from her. Then the screaming from him.

"I didn't mean for it to happen."

A roll of the thumb. A small sheet of paper. An accident.

She looked down at her arm, at the waxy skin raised and roiled. It started on the back of her hand and made a skeleton imprint of her bone structure. Then it continued over her wrist and sucked the meat from her forearm.

"Can I see the lighter?"

Chelsea reached into her pocket and set it next to the ashes on the table between them. He thanked her and told her to leave the box and the lighter until their next session.

"Are you comfortable with that?" he asked. Chelsea nodded.

***

In her apartment, Chelsea set the kettle to boil and grabbed a teabag from the drawer. She set the candle on the table and paced around the apartment. Once the kettle had whistled, and she thought of Lauren, and the steam had reached her nose, and the lavender had calmed her, she went to the cabinet in the bathroom, took another from her stash of yellow lighters, flicked it on, and watched it burn.

Good Life
Matt Pogemiller

Roger barrels ahead along the trail. He stops at the edge of the tall grass, sniffs along the ground for a few seconds, then lumbers on ahead and around a curve in the path. You can hear his rapid panting even though you can't see him anymore. The sun is high and relentless, absolutely baking the top of your head. You need to get to the timberline. Your skin feels like it is being cooked, and you are exposed to everything and everyone out here. You are both in dire need of water. You stop, stand unmoving and quiet, and listen for the sound of the river, which you think must be close. But the only sound is the tall fescue rustling in the wind.

You round the corner of the path and almost trip over Roger. The dog stands rigid, alert and still. The mane on the back of his black neckline is slightly raised into a bristled ridge. But he isn't making a sound, no low growl, which means he has determined that whatever he has seen is merely worth keeping an eye on. You look towards the spot he is fixed on and see the top of the grass bending sideways as something moves away from the trail. Probably a raccoon or possum, maybe even a stray cat. Roger is well trained, and he has always had good instincts. His behavior tells you there is nothing to be gained by chasing this animal. His ears relax. He sits and turns towards you.

"Good boy," you say, and Roger resumes panting while you scratch the top of his head. He grunts when it is time to start moving again. His legs have stiffened in the short time that he has been sitting, and you know that he is in pain.

"Good dog," you say, and Roger picks up the pace to show you he has heard.

* * *

What sticks with you, then? What do you remember?

The ruined, crumbling mansion in the woods. Somewhere in Michigan, way north. The stone staircase, covered in moss, leading up to thin air thirty feet from the ground. Unsafe to be up there. You climbed every step, stood at the top and looked down into the abyss. Who else had walked those stairs? What kind of lives had been lived in that place? Off in the distance a grayish box. Some small structure, maybe an old shed or garage? But when you climbed back down the stairs to investigate, it turned out to be a marble mausoleum, which showed surprisingly few signs of wear despite being exposed to the elements for decades. You looked through the dirty pane of glass and saw a ceramic white hand suspended by a thin, almost invisible wire hanging from the ceiling. What did it mean? Who would choose this as their eternal symbol?

The boy on the sandbar in the middle of the Mississippi. Maybe fourteen or fifteen, shirtless, barefoot, staring at the water. Something was off. Roger didn't like the area. He couldn't sit still. He whined and circled around you. You crouched low along the edge of the water and watched the boy for an hour, but he hardly moved. Eventually a small flat-bottomed boat with two men appeared from upriver, and the boy jumped in when they pulled up to the edge of the sand. The three of them behaved as if they were familiar with each other. You spent the next few days trying to understand what set of circumstances led up to this scene, and then for many months after that you did not see another human being.

The black bear swam across the lake with her cubs, all of them exhaling audibly, shaking off on the shore, unaware that you were watching from the deck of the red house just fifty yards away. The roof at that place had mostly caved in, and when it rained you and Roger either sat in the corner and waited it out or you just got wet. In the warmer months you used to sit outside on the green picnic table and let the rain come down.

No one else will remember any of this, of course, after you are gone.

* * *

Roger finds the cabin first. You hear him coming back down the trail towards you, and when he reaches you, he brushes against your legs, his tail wagging furiously. He sits and smiles, tongue hanging out and dripping. He's waiting for your approval.

"You find something?" you ask, and Roger closes his mouth for a moment, looks serious.

Yes.

"Show me," you say, and then add, "Slow, quiet."

You follow him down the trail for a few minutes until he suddenly turns, stops at a clearing, and looks up the ridge. When you get closer you see indentations in the grass, about five feet apart, leading up the slope. Dirt shows through the ruts in spots. Somebody used to have a reason to drive up this hill.

"It's an old dirt road," you say to Roger, who makes eye contact and waits for a different tone in your voice to tell him what to do. You scan the area, but it's too dense to see much, just a pair of grown over tire tracks leading through the trees up the hill. No smell or sound that indicates anybody is around.

"Go ahead," you say to Roger. "Slow."

The cabin has clearly been abandoned for many years. Ivy snakes around the exterior, hugging the rotted siding and choking the window frames. The roof is covered in moss but intact. The front steps have collapsed, a small evergreen rises in the middle of the scattered wood. Most of the porch floorboards have rotted through and you can see right through to the black earth.

You walk closer to the cabin, cautious but also fascinated. There has to be a better way inside than through this tangled mess in the front. Roger has disappeared, which is odd. You had expected him to strut around and brag about his discovery. You call his name, and after a minute he appears from around the backside of the cabin. He stops in front of you, and you stoop down to pet the top of his head. His eyes are alert, he has found something else he thinks you need to see. You reach underneath his chin and scratch the graying fur on the bottom of his lower jaw. His nose is cool to the touch. You run your hands along the sides of his snout and feel that it is soaking wet.

The cabin is not what he wants to show you.

"Water," you say, and the dog turns and runs back around the side of the cabin.

* * *

The lookout tower that you found out west was your favorite spot. It took all day to convince Roger to climb up all those stairs. He was terrified of the space in between the steps. The little shelf with all the instructional books about forest fires. The topographical map of the surrounding area taped to the wall with the red pins lined up along the side, waiting to indicate danger. Notebooks with neat, slanted handwriting laid out journal-style, the meticulous documentation of the last fire lookout that had lived in the tower. Coordinates, notes in the side margins about conversations with other lookouts on the walkie. Three pairs of different sized binoculars sitting on the small table by the twin bed, seemingly waiting for you to take over the duty.

How many hours did you and Roger sit, looking out at those trees and mountains? Was it something like peace that you found? Do you remember the little jolt in your gut the first time you spotted the trail of smoke coming from the trees off in the distance?

From the safety of the tower, the fires were amazing to watch. There didn't seem to be any discernible pattern. They came and went, sometimes intensifying to the point that you thought you might have to flee, but then the wind would shift, or the rains would come, and you'd forget about it. You'd hike down the mountain with Roger in the afternoon to get out of the hot tower, and you'd both sit by the stream and fish with the pole that was left behind in the lookout.

What else?

There was something calling you back east, even though you already knew there was nothing left. On the way, the storms in the plains were terrifying. You remember cowering under an overpass with Roger as baseball-sized hail thundered against the concrete above and around you.

Your childhood home was virtually unrecognizable, almost fully torn apart. The split-level at the end of the block was the only house left that still had a roof. The houses farther down toward the cul-de-sac were being completely reclaimed by nature. The trees looked like they were slowly consuming the wood and concrete in a silent march towards something only they understood.

* * *

A hundred yards behind the cabin is a stream with clear, cool water flowing rapidly towards the river. The sound of the water is beautiful, but you resist the urge to drop to your knees and drink. You know there might be bacteria or parasites. You'll have to be patient. You have a filter in your backpack, and some purifying tablets.

Roger can't help himself. He crouches down and laps at the water, even though he has had plenty already.

"Easy," you say. "You'll get sick if you drink too much." You unzip your backpack and pull out the larger of the two canteens that you carry with you. You fill it up, drop two tablets into the water, and screw the cap back on. Roger follows you back towards the cabin. You find a low window in the back, and you peek through it before you stoop, pick

Roger up, and lift him over the ledge. You set him down gently on the wooden flooring, but he still lets out a grunt. You heft yourself up to climb in and look around. The place is a time capsule, by appearance untouched for as long as you've been alive. A wicker chair in the corner of the main room. A bookcase crammed with rotting old newspapers and paperbacks. A faded black and red dartboard hanging on the wall. A circular table in the middle of the room with an empty glass vase sitting atop it. A small room adjacent with a box frame and mattress. The wall above the bed bare save for a lone, framed picture of a beautiful brunette woman in a sleeveless dress, smiling at the camera, sitting on a chair on the tidy front porch of the cabin you are standing in, a lifetime later.

Roger inspects the corners, sniffs the newspapers and the chair, then lays down on the dusty rug underneath the table and watches you.

"You like it here," you say, and the dog continues to watch you, his ears at ease. You are making a statement, not asking. He is nearing the end of his trailblazing days. You know his hips are not in the best shape. There is the stream, no doubt a river nearby, plenty of fish and water. No sign of other humans or any trouble, although you understand that can always change.

You wait another twenty minutes, then you unscrew the canteen lid and take a long, slow drink of water. You go into the other room and swat some dust off the bed sheet before you decide to let it go, and then you lay down, exhausted.

How long can a person keep doing this? What are you going to do when he's not around?

"We'll stay," you call out to Roger in the other room, and you hear him roll over on his side and sigh.

* * *

One of your strongest memories, then, of course. You woke after what seemed to have been a long period of blackness. You were in a school classroom, or what used to serve as one. The small chairs with attached desks. The hardbound math textbooks scattered everywhere across the filthy floor. On the blackboard someone had written in chalk, "*Welcome to the Good Life!*". You stared for a long time at a dusty radiator in the corner of the room, and you were confused. Also, impossibly thirsty.

Outside of the school and down the road, then. You weren't sure what had happened. Any sort of recent memory was a blank. You didn't know what town you were in or how you had gotten there.

You smelled the fire before you saw it. You turned and saw the smoke in the distance. Towards the west, outside of town. Unmistakable. You were trying not to panic but you needed water and you needed to get out of there fast.

Through the long grass of the small park, then. Blurry, red, bubbled mists formed at the edges of your vision. You ran your hands across your forehead and looked at your palms and you saw you were somehow bleeding. You stopped and kneeled by the fountain, stuck your face in the brown water and took huge gulps, knowing it was probably a mistake, knowing you'd just vomit it up and feel even more thirsty.

Along the railroad tracks towards the industrial buildings, then. For the first time you felt the heat of the fire behind you. A young black lab suddenly appeared and ran along next to you. Rib cage visible, poking through the fur on the dog's sides. Through a gap in the buildings you saw a bridge, and you both veered towards it. A group of deer burst past you, and the lab, startled, barked after them. They branched off to the right of the bridge as you got closer, and you and the dog followed.

The river within sight, then. You did not turn around to look but you could feel the heat had intensified. You needed to get into the water. You crashed through the underbrush, the dog still there beside you. Against the rocks along the shore, you saw an upended, rusty canoe, anchored by a stake in the sand. You bent down, heaving, as you flipped it over, then you pushed it a few feet into the water and turned back. The dog was there, panting furiously, whining.

How was it still alive? It couldn't weigh more than forty pounds. Half the weight it should have been.

"Come on," you said, and you turned the canoe sideways so the dog could jump in, but it backed away and barked at you.

Huge, black, billowing clouds plumed skyward back towards the direction you had just come from. The fire was now audible, roaring like a blowtorch.

There wasn't much more time, then, so you had moved towards the dog, intending to pick it up and put it in the canoe. But the dog jumped back again and wouldn't let you get close enough to grab it.

You had to go. You pushed the canoe towards the middle of the river and jumped in, almost tipping it over. You reached your arm down and used it like a paddle, splashing clumsily towards the deeper water, where the current would take you south.

Why were you weeping, then? Why had the world turned hostile, sinister?

You turned back to the shore. The dog was there, pacing frantically back and forth and whining.

"Come on!" you screamed. And then you sat down in the canoe. Blood from your forehead dripped down onto your nose, and you closed your eyes.

How could anyone survive in a place like this?

You laid down and rested then, defeated. The aluminum ridge along the bottom of the canoe poked into your spine. The roar from the fire was astonishing. A loud booming sound erupted from the direction of the industrial buildings, but you kept your eyes shut, content to drift.

Something splashed off to the side of the canoe. You sat up and looked, and the dog was ten feet away, swimming low in the water, making chuffing, sneezing noises as it paddled towards you, eyes wide open and pleading. You rose to your knees and reached out as it got closer, then scooped and lifted it into the canoe in one motion. You could see then that it was a male. The dog shook himself off and then collapsed on his side, drained.

"Good boy," you said, and the dog barked in response.

"Roger that," you said.

Untitled 2
Spike Dawkins

Spike Dawkins (she/her) is a writer with an interest in photography. Her novel, Lost Boys, was shortlisted for the Crime Writers' Association Debut Dagger Award in 2017. She lives in Iowa City.

Rachel J. Sharkey (she/her) is originally from Calgary, Alberta, Canada, and came to Iowa City via Montreal. She works as a neuroscientist and is not sure where academia will take her next, but she hopes it's somewhere cold.

Ross T. Byers (he/him) The entity referred to as Ross T. Byers seeped into this reality during a rare celestial convergence. Taking the guise of a horror writer, it patched together a skinsuit and has walked among you ever since, sowing nightmares in the unwary populace through the medium of prose.

Erin Casey (she/her) is an urban/YA fantasy writer and author of The Purple Door District series. She's a founder and the Director of the Writers' Rooms and an advocate for mental health. When not writing, she dotes on her flock of birds. To learn more about her, her books, and her birds, visit erincasey.org.

Theodore Michelet Sterling (he/him) lives in Iowa with his wife, two sons, and an indeterminate number of cats (usually three).

Freddy Niagara Fonseca (he/him), poet, dramatic reader has read poems in five languages. He authored "This Enduring Gift," and "The Bomb That Blew Up God." Freddy performed in public numerous times in his Candlelight Reading Series, presenting World Poetry of all eras with musicians, dancers, and actors. He lives in Iowa.

Laura Goldman Weinberg (she/her) is multi-talented and multi-creative. She is a writer, songwriter, poet, and visual artist. Her art, songs, and writings are universal, recognizing the Oneness everywhere. She allows the creative energy to flow through her and continues to create in various forms with the hope of inspiring and uplifting others.

Daniel Brawner (he/him) is a humor columnist for The Mount Vernon/Lisbon SUN and The Marion Times. He is the author of the mystery novel "Employment is Murder" and is currently pursuing his passion for making independent films. Dan lives in Iowa City with his wife, Laura Rigal.

Kristine Perkins' (she/her) work has appeared in Not Deer Magazine, Local Honey | Midwest, Running Wild Press and the Same blog. She lives in Iowa.

Jill Cronbaugh (she/her) hates writing author bios. Her first piece was a short-story at the age of 6 about the time her grandpa took her to steal some field corn for her pony. The reviews were great! It delighted her grandfather & embarrassed her mother –- all-in-all, a job well done!

Megan Walsh (she/her) is a writer in Iowa City, IA. When she's not distracted by the dishes or her dog or organizing her pens or alphabetizing her books, she's probably writing (or reading or talking to her plants or reorganizing her apartment).

Matt Pogemiller (he/him) lives in Iowa City, Iowa, with his wife (Deb), son (Owen), and dog (Pippa). He is currently working on a master's degree in English and hopes to teach full-time upon completion of his degree. This is his first published story.

ALSO CHECK OUT
THE WRITERS' ROOMS

the writers' rooms
www.TheWritersRooms.org

OUR ROOTS

The Writers' Rooms began in late 2015 under the welcoming umbrella of the Iowa Writers' House. We had a simple mission in mind: create a free, accessible community to Iowan writers. The Violet Realm, our sci-fi/fantasy Room, started it all. For two years we incubated under the IWH and learned what our community needed to foster creative minds. It became apparent that if we were going to support our writers, it would be through a community- and crowd-sourced endeavor.

OUR MISSION

Our writing community has the amazing benefit of a massive collection of backgrounds, experiences, and viewpoints. The Writers' Rooms endeavors to bring these wonderful ideas together and help all writers with their craft. We strive to encourage and foster community-based knowledge to help lead literary sessions and provide a safe, positive writing environment. Our Rooms are moderated by both our Concierges and the members of our community. Community-led sessions tap into the wealth of our collective knowledge, allowing our writers to both share their own experiences and learn from other attendees.

The Rooms can't exist without you and your passion and experience!

OUR PEOPLE

Concierge members come from the writing community. All of our current concierges were interested in their topics and became knowledgeable about their genre through reading, writing, and taking lessons of their own. Anyone interested in leading a particular genre- or topic-based Room is welcome to e-mail us at welcome@thewritersrooms.org.

The rest of the Room membership comes from eager writer minds who want to know more about a particular genre or topic. Some have even graciously led lessons for us. We're always looking for more people to share their expertise.

Find out more at: Facebook (IAWritersRooms), and follow us on Instagram (@WritersRooms) and Twitter (@IAWritersRooms).

Donations

The Writers' Rooms are and will always be free to the public.
Everything we do is out-of-pocket from our Director and Concierges, funded by the sale of anthologies and merchandise, or the product of generous donations from the community.
All proceeds are used wholly for The Writers' Rooms' day-to-day operational expenses, to fund event appearances and community outreach, and to publish our annual Community Anthology.

Donate through…
PayPal! Paypal.me/thewritersrooms
CashApp! Cash.app/$thewritersrooms
Ko-fi! Ko-fi.com/thewritersrooms

Purchase our Anthologies! *thewritersrooms.org/store*
Prefer eBooks? All of our anthologies (A New Adventure, Writers of the Depths, and Writers of the Aether) are available for purchase on our website.

Check out our Teespring! *the-writers-rooms.creator-spring.com*
Here you can buy a host of different items from The Writers' Rooms and specific Rooms, like our TWR Pride shirt or Make It Gay mug! Not seeing something you want? Submit a request to welcome@thewritersrooms.org!

Subscribe to our Patreon! *www.patreon.com/TheWritersRooms*
This subscription service allows you to support The Writers' Rooms on a monthly basis, for as little as $1 per month. You will be featured on our Donate page at www.thewritersrooms.org/donate. Keep an eye out for more Patron perks soon!

Thank you! We can't do this without you!

www.ingramcontent.com/pod-product-compliance
Lightning Source LLC
Chambersburg PA
CBHW030754110726
47900CB00008B/2605